Puppy School

Neil, Emily and Sam hurried towards the excitable Dalmatian and her owner. As soon as she scented them, Dotty started pulling at her lead and barking loudly. Neil chuckled. Dotty was a beautiful dog; well-proportioned and slender, with long, elegant legs and a sleek white coat covered in glossy black spots.

"Hello, Mr Hamley," Neil called as they approached. His eyes widened in amazement as he looked at Dotty more closely. He nudged his sister and said, "I think Dotty's going to be a mum!"

Titles in the Puppy Patrol *series*

More Puppy Patrol stories follow soon

Puppy Patrol
Puppy School

Jenny Dale

Illustrated by

Mick Reid

A Working Partners Book

MACMILLAN CHILDREN'S BOOKS

Special thanks to Narinder Dhami

First published 1998 by Macmillan Children's Books
a division of Macmillan Publishers Limited
25 Eccleston Place, London SW1W 9NF
Basingstoke and Oxford
www.macmillan.co.uk

Associated companies throughout the world

Created by Working Partners Limited
London W12 7QY

ISBN 0 330 37040 5

9 8

A CIP catalogue record for this book is available from
the British Library.

Typeset in Bookman Old Style by SX Composing DTP, Rayleigh, Essex
Printed and bound in Great Britain by Mackays of Chatham plc, Kent

Chapter One

"Brr, it's freezing!" Neil Parker complained, as he and his younger sister Emily walked briskly across the field, their breath steaming in the frosty morning air. "Did you notice how cold it was in school yesterday? I reckon Mr Grundy's turned the heating down again!"

"He's so mean!" Emily said indignantly. Then she began to laugh. "And so grumpy! Julie and I call him Grumpy Grundy!"

Neil grinned. "Good one, Em. He's been at Meadowbank for a couple of months now, and I haven't seen him smile once, yet."

"Maybe he's not a head teacher at all," Emily said, shaking her dark brown hair out of her eyes. "Maybe he's really an alien who's come to conquer Earth, and take over our minds."

"Well, he won't have much trouble with yours!" Neil teased her. He dodged a playful smack from his sister, then turned round to check where Sam, his black and white Border collie, had got to. It was Saturday morning, and they were taking Sam for a quick walk up on the ridgeway before breakfast. It was one of Neil's favourite dog-walking routes near their home in Compton.

Sam had stopped to sniff at something interesting on the footpath.

"Here, boy!" Neil called. Sam immediately

bounded towards him, wagging his feathery plume of a tail. He was a handsome dog, with a thick, shaggy coat and dark eyes that were always alert and eager. Neil bent down and patted him, thinking, as he always did, how impossible it was that Sam could really be ill when he looked so bright and lively.

"Good boy!"

Neil had to keep a sharp eye on Sam. The collie had recently been diagnosed with a heart murmur, after collapsing at the end of an important Agility competition. Sam had won the contest, but that was hardly any consolation for Neil. One day, Sam's heart would simply give up, and Neil hated to think about it. For now, though, Sam was a healthy, happy dog and the apple of Neil Parker's eye.

"I don't see why Mr Grundy has to be so miserable," Emily persisted, as they walked up the footpath with Sam. "Anybody would think he didn't like children."

"He probably doesn't," Neil replied. "And I bet he doesn't like dogs, either." To Neil, anyone who didn't like dogs was definitely a bit suspect.

Dogs were the most important thing in the world to Neil. He sometimes wondered if that was because he lived at King Street Kennels, or if he had just been born loving dogs. Neil liked to think that maybe it was a bit of both.

King Street Kennels was run by Neil and Emily's parents, Bob and Carole Parker. They took in boarders, but they also cared for abandoned dogs in the rescue centre. Neil was surrounded by dogs, day and night, and that was just the way he liked it.

Emily bent down to pat Sam's head. "Mr Grundy certainly doesn't like guinea-pigs, anyway. When he came into our classroom last week, he made me put Mortimer's cage outside in the corridor!"

Neil couldn't help smiling at his sister's tone of voice. "I think he should be in the army," he said, thinking about the new head's tall, straight-backed figure and toothbrush moustache. "I keep expecting him to shout 'Quick march!' when we go into assembly!"

"He's got a loud voice too," Emily added, as they reached the ridgeway. "You can hear him shouting right across the playground."

"Maybe he'll settle down soon. You know how dogs sometimes take a while to settle in when they first arrive at the kennels."

Emily raised her eyebrows. "What kind of dog would Mr Grundy be then?"

"A Rottweiler?" Neil suggested, with a grin.

Emily giggled. Then she pointed along the footpath. "Look, isn't that Mr Hamley and Dotty?"

Neil squinted along the ridgeway. A man with a Dalmatian on a lead was walking along some distance ahead of them.

"Yes, it is. C'mon, let's say hello. I haven't seen Dotty for ages."

Mr Hamley was Neil's teacher at Meadowbank Primary School, and his Dalmatian, Dotty, was one of the most appealing, but also one of the naughtiest dogs that Neil had ever known. She had been such a boisterous bundle of chaos that the Hamleys had considered giving her away. Neil had been determined to train her to follow instructions, and his efforts, along with his father's obedience classes, had paid off.

Neil, Emily and Sam hurried towards the crazy Dalmatian. As soon as she scented them, she started pulling at her lead and barking loudly. Neil chuckled. Although she was much better behaved now, Dotty's training hadn't worked miracles! But she was a beautiful dog; well-proportioned and slender, with long, elegant legs and a sleek white coat covered in glossy black spots.

5

"Hello, Mr Hamley," Neil called as they approached. He could see Dotty more closely now, and his eyes widened in amazement. It wasn't always easy to tell when a bitch was expecting puppies, but Neil could see that Dotty was. He nudged his sister as they walked up to Mr Hamley and the Dalmatian. "I think Dotty's going to be a mum!"

Emily hadn't noticed, but now she looked thrilled. "That's great!"

Neil knew what the signs were. He had helped out at the birth of Jake, Sam's son. Jake was still with his mother, Delilah, but as soon as he was old enough he'd be coming to live at King Street – a new puppy for Neil. Neil had never looked forward to anything more in his life.

"Hello, Neil, Emily." Paul Hamley smiled, then almost fell flat on his face as Dotty lunged towards them, taking her owner with her. "Down, Dotty!" he said firmly. Dotty dropped to the ground reluctantly, every muscle tensed, her liquid brown eyes staring hopefully at Neil and Emily. Emily knelt down and put her arms round the dog's neck, and Dotty wagged her tail happily, trying to lick Emily's nose.

"Is Dotty having pups, Mr Hamley?" Neil just

managed to stop himself from sounding surprised. He knew how much of a handful Dotty could be, and he couldn't help wondering how the Hamleys, who also had a new baby, would cope.

"Yes, she is," Mr Hamley said, beaming proudly at the excited Dalmatian. The teacher was nicknamed Smiler because his teaching manner could hardly be described as fun-filled. When he was with Dottie, though, he was a lot more approachable. "They're due in two weeks' time, around the 15th. She looks well, doesn't she?"

"Brilliant," Neil agreed, kneeling down beside Emily to stroke the dog's beautifully marked coat. Delighted, Dotty put out her tongue, and licked Neil's hand. "I didn't know you were going to breed from Dotty, Mr Hamley."

"Well, we weren't planning to," Mr Hamley replied, "but a friend of mine has a Dalmatian called Ainsley, and he persuaded us to, er . . ."

"Mate the dogs?" Neil suggested in a businesslike fashion.

"Well, yes." Mr Hamley looked a little embarrassed. Neil smiled to himself. He wasn't embarrassed at all. Having puppies was a perfectly natural thing for a dog to do, and Dotty seemed to be thriving. She was now sniffing Sam, and rubbing noses with the collie.

"Are you going to keep the puppies, Mr Hamley?" Emily asked curiously. The Hamleys could barely cope with Dotty as it was, let alone a bunch of lively little puppies.

Mr Hamley looked alarmed. "No, no, but we'll find them good homes, of course. To be honest, we thought it might calm Dottie down if she became a mum."

Neil and Emily looked down at Dottie, who was now jumping round Mr Hamley's legs playing hide and seek with Sam, and then at each other. They both knew what the other was thinking. Some hope!

"You must be very busy with your baby," Emily said politely, as a rather flustered Mr Hamley ordered Dotty to sit.

He nodded. "Yes, and the autumn term's always the busiest too, what with all the preparations for Christmas. I'm involved in setting up the evening classes which are starting at the school next term too, and with a new head teacher as well . . ." Mr Hamley's voice trailed away.

Neil suddenly noticed how tired he was looking and realized that it must be hard for everyone, including the teachers, to adapt to a new head teacher. Especially a head teacher like Mr Grundy.

"Well, I must get off home." Mr Hamley seemed to pull himself up sharply, as if he'd realized that he shouldn't be complaining about his workload to two pupils. "I'll see you on Monday. Come along, Dotty."

"Just a minute, Mr Hamley," Neil said quickly. He'd suddenly thought of a rather good way of helping the teacher and Dotty out.

"Yes?" Mr Hamley turned back, looking rather grumpy himself.

"I could walk Dotty for you sometimes," Neil suggested. "Would that help?"

Mr Hamley seemed taken aback for a moment. "That's a very generous offer, Neil. Are you sure you wouldn't mind?" Then he laughed, as he looked at Neil's eager face. "No, of course you wouldn't!"

Neil arranged to call for Dotty on Monday after school. Then he and Emily said their goodbyes and headed back to King Street Kennels.

"I wish Mr Hamley was our head teacher instead of Mr Grundy," Emily sighed. "I wonder why he didn't get the job? Mrs Hamley told Mum he'd applied for it."

Neil shrugged. "Obviously Grumpy Grundy had something that Smiler didn't."

"Like what?"

"Mum said she reckons the governors wanted someone who could save the school some money. Haven't you noticed how Mr Grundy's been going round all the classrooms, counting everything and checking how many exercise books we use? We never get new pencils or rubbers any more."

"I'm down to my last well-chewed stub!" Emily snorted as they arrived home.

The Parkers lived in the countryside on the outskirts of town. The kennel buildings were at the back of the house, built around a square courtyard. It was just as well they had no close neighbours, because there was a constant sound of dogs barking. There were other buildings too; Red's Barn, where Bob Parker held his twice-weekly obedience classes, and also the small block of kennels which housed the rescue centre.

Even though it was still early, King Street was already open for business. Neil and Emily headed for the kennels office, while Sam trotted off to have a drink and then a snooze under his favourite hedge in the back garden. Kate McGuire, the kennel maid, was in the office, looking pale and very sorry for herself, and blowing her nose on a handkerchief.

"Hello, Kate," Neil said with a frown. "What's wrong?"

Kate attempted a smile. "Your dad told me to go home," she said in a hoarse voice. "I think I'm getting this flu that's been going round."

Neil and Emily looked sympathetic. They all liked Kate. She was great with the dogs, and was almost like one of the family.

"I'm going to run Kate home in a moment or two." Bob Parker, a large, well-built man with thick dark hair and a shaggy beard, came up behind them. "Your mother's doing the morning feeds by herself in Block One, so if you two want to give her a hand . . ."

"Sure," Neil said, delighted. "Where's Squirt?"

As if on cue, his little sister Sarah appeared.

"Can I come with you to take Kate home, Dad?" she asked.

Bob shook his head. "We don't want you coming down with flu too, sweetheart."

"Poor Kate," Sarah said, patting the kennel maid's arm. "I'll paint you a picture of all the dogs in the kennels. That'll make you feel better."

Neil and Emily grinned at each other. Sarah's response to any crisis, big or small, was to paint a picture – usually of a dog.

"Come on, Squirt," Neil said. "You can help us with the morning feeds."

Neil, Sarah and Emily crossed the courtyard and stepped into Kennel Block One. Both kennel blocks were light and spacious with ten pens on each side of a central aisle. Their mother was unlocking the pen of a large black mongrel, a bowl of dog biscuits in her hand. Duke had been left there a couple of days previously by his owners, Mr and Mrs Carter, who had gone on holiday. The dog was slumped in a corner, looking miserable, but as Carole walked into the pen, he climbed to his feet.

12

"Guess what, Mum?" Neil called. "Dotty's having pups!"

"Really?" Carole Parker raised her eyebrows. She was a tall, striking-looking woman, with short black hair and a brisk, no-nonsense manner. "Well, let's hope it calms her down a bit, although I wouldn't bet on it!"

"That's what we thought," Emily laughed.

"More puppies!" Sarah said, delighted. She had been thrilled when Sam and Delilah's puppies had been born, although she hadn't been at the birth. "I hope Dotty has lots and lots!"

"I don't," Neil said quickly. "I don't think Mr Hamley could cope!"

"Maybe he and Dotty will surprise us all!" their mother said with a grin. She was inside Duke's pen now, and the dog was on his feet, muscles tensed. He looked nervous. "Easy, boy," Carole said soothingly. "I've just come to give you some food. Nobody's going to hurt you."

For some reason the dog began growling, a low, menacing sound deep in the back of his throat.

Neil began to feel alarmed. "What's the matter with him?" he muttered to Emily. "He was OK

13

when I fed him yesterday." The dog hadn't been particularly friendly the previous evening, but Neil hadn't been surprised. Some dogs took longer to settle in at the kennels than others.

Carole Parker put the dish down, still talking to the dog in a reassuring voice. Suddenly Duke leaped forward, his jaws drawn back in a vicious snarl. As Neil, Emily and Sarah watched, wide-eyed with horror, the dog pounced on their mother and sank his teeth into her hand.

Carole Parker screamed.

Chapter Two

Neil warned Emily and Sarah in a low voice to stay absolutely still and quiet as their mother stood up and hesitantly stepped out of the pen, her face pale and drawn. Almost as soon as he had bitten her, Duke had slunk off, his tail between his legs. He now sat hunched in the corner of his pen, staring at the floor.

Neil ran over to his mother, his heart thumping with anxiety. He pulled off his sweatshirt and held it out to her. She immediately wrapped it tightly round her right hand, trying to stem the flow of blood.

"Dad!" Emily yelled frantically, racing out of the kennel block towards the house. Sarah began to cry.

"What's the matter?" A moment later Bob appeared in the open doorway, with Kate close behind him. "Carole, are you all right? What happened?"

"I went in to feed Duke . . ." Carole was obviously in a good deal of pain, and had to force the words out, ". . . and he – he attacked me."

"He just seemed to go mad," Neil muttered. He stared at the dog, who had retreated into his basket, looking as if he knew well enough that he had done wrong.

"Did he break the skin?" Bob asked, gently trying to take his wife's hand. "Is there any blood?"

Carole nodded and winced, biting down hard on her lip, as Bob unwrapped the sweatshirt. Horrified, Neil caught a brief glimpse of blood pouring from a large wound in his mother's hand. It looked even worse close-up. Bob, seeing the look on Neil's face, quickly wrapped the sweatshirt back into place.

"I'd better get you to Casualty," he said. "You're going to need stitches."

"Mummy!" Sarah wailed, sobbing even harder.

"I'm fine, sweetheart," Carole said, making an effort to sound calm, but Neil had never seen her look so white and shocked before. "The hospital will soon sort me out."

"I'll stay with the kids while you two go to Casualty," Kate said, putting her arm round Sarah.

"But you're not well—" Carole began.

"Just go," Kate said firmly, fishing in the pocket of her jeans for a clean handkerchief to wipe Sarah's face. "We'll be fine."

"Thanks, Kate." Bob put his arm round his wife, and led her away. "And none of you are to go into that dog's pen under any circumstances," he added sternly over his shoulder.

Neil felt sick as he watched his mother and father hurry off. It was distressing on the rare occasions when a dog suddenly turned vicious, especially when there didn't seem to be a rational explanation.

"Come on, Neil," Kate called as she led Emily and Sarah towards the house. "Let's go inside and have a cup of tea. Then we'll feed the rest of the dogs."

Neil glanced round the kennel block before he followed the others. Most of the pens were occupied, but all the dogs were strangely subdued, sensing that something was wrong. Duke was slumped in his basket, head between his paws, looking very sorry for himself.

"Why did you do it, boy?" Neil asked softly, wondering what was going to happen next. He knew that the police could take the owners of a dangerous dog to court, and that could sometimes mean the dog being put down. It would probably all depend on whether or not Duke had ever done anything like it before.

It was around lunchtime when Neil heard the sound of the family Range Rover pulling onto the driveway outside the house. Anxiously he ran outside, followed by the others.

"Don't worry," Bob said cheerfully, as he helped Carole out of the car. "Your mum has been well looked after at the hospital, and she's fine."

Carole's hand was heavily bandaged and in a sling, but Neil was relieved to see that she looked less ill, and had regained some colour in her face.

"Of course I'm fine!" she said, putting her other arm round Sarah. "Now why don't you come inside and we'll have some lunch, while your dad runs poor old Kate home?"

"Oh, I can walk," Kate said heroically, sneezing into a tissue. "Bob must want his lunch."

"Lunch can wait. You look awful, Kate," Bob told her.

"Thanks," Kate replied, grimacing.

"Can I come, Dad?" Neil asked. He wanted to have a private chat with his father about Duke.

Bob nodded, and the three of them climbed into the Range Rover. Neil told Kate and Bob that Dotty was expecting pups, but he didn't mention Duke until they'd dropped Kate off and were heading back home. Then he took a deep breath and turned to his dad.

"Dad, what's going to happen to Duke?"

His father looked grim. "I don't know, Neil. There's not a lot we can do about it until his owners come back, anyway."

"I don't understand why he suddenly turned on Mum like that."

Bob shrugged. "There are different reasons why dogs become aggressive. Duke might have been abused when he was a pup, or it may be something to do with the way his present owners treat him."

"Will he have to be put down?" Neil persisted.

"It's hard to say." Bob swung the Range Rover expertly down the narrow country lane. "We'd have to take the owners to court if we think the dog should be put down, and let the magistrate decide."

Neil paused. He hated the thought of a young, healthy dog being put down, but seeing Duke attack his mum had terrified him. Duke was dangerous and unpredictable.

"Do you think he's bitten anyone before?"

"It's possible. But if he has, it was appallingly irresponsible of the Carters not to let us know."

His father sounded really angry. They relied on the owners to give them as much information as they possibly could about their dogs. If they were less than truthful, this could be the result.

"Anyway," Bob went on, "I want to stop off at the police station and report this to Sergeant Moorhead. That makes it official."

Neil nodded. Sergeant Moorhead had been involved in a previous case involving a dangerous dog at King Street Kennels. Skye, a rough collie, had been wrongly accused of savaging sheep, and Neil and Emily had found the real culprit. This time, though, Neil thought, there was no doubt who the guilty party was . . .

"You were right to come and report it," Sergeant Moorhead remarked as he finished taking down Bob and Neil's statement. Neil had been interviewed because he had seen the attack take place, and the policeman also wanted to speak to Carole herself. "What do you want to do now?"

Bob frowned. "We'll have to wait until the Carters come back from holiday, of course."

Sergeant Moorhead nodded. He was middle-aged, with short grey hair and a calm, controlled manner. "Yes, but are you prepared to keep the dog at the kennels, or do you want me to take charge of him?"

"You mean you'll take him into custody, like you did with Skye?" Bob asked.

"We haven't got any room in the police kennels at the moment," Sergeant Moorhead replied, "but I expect the RSPCA would take him in."

"There doesn't seem much point in moving the dog around." Bob made up his mind quickly. "We'll keep him until his owners come back, as long as my wife's happy with that."

Neil felt a pang of unhappiness as he and his father left the police station. It was extremely rare for any dog to stay at King Street Kennels under such a cloud. Neil couldn't help feeling depressed on Duke's behalf. The Carters were certainly in for a shock when they got back from their holiday.

"Dotty's *pregnant*?" Chris Wilson said incredulously, as he and Neil cycled through the school gates on Monday morning. "Old Smiler's going to have his hands full, isn't he?"

Neil nodded. "Especially if Dotty's pups take after their mother!" he pointed out.

Chris laughed. He was Neil's best mate, and they looked very much alike. They even had the same dark brown spiky hair.

"I noticed Smiler was looking even more fed up than usual, but I thought that was probably because of Mr Grundy!"

"I wonder what surprises Grumpy's got lined up for us today?" Neil remarked, as they went over to the bike sheds.

"Grumpy Grundy? Hey, I like it!" Chris said with a grin.

"It's what Emily calls him," Neil replied. "I think the name really suits him!"

"By the way, how's your mum?"

"She's all right," Neil replied. Carole Parker had spent most of the weekend resting, but that morning she'd been up to get them off to school, looking almost back to her usual self. "She can't use her hand that much though, and Kate's got flu. I hope she's back soon."

His mother hadn't objected to Duke staying

on at King Street, but Neil had noticed that she hadn't been out into the kennels all weekend, and Bob, with help from Neil and Emily, had done all the feeding and walking of the dogs. It was tough on his father, Neil thought, because he and Emily couldn't help out that much when they were stuck in school all day. But Bob hadn't been too keen on Emily's suggestion that they should both take the week off school to help out at home.

Chris glanced across the playground, and nudged Neil in the ribs. "Here comes Grumpy," he whispered.

Mr Grundy was striding across the play-ground, tall and stern, briefcase under his arm, glaring at any child who happened to get in his way.

"Do you think he *ever* smiles?" Chris whispered.

Neil shook his head. "I don't think he'd smile even if he won the lottery!"

"Who's won the lottery then?" said a voice close to Neil's ear. "The Puppy Patrol?"

Neil looked round, and saw Hasheem Lindon, who was in his class. Hasheem was always teasing Neil about his obsession with all things doggy. The Parker family was now known throughout Compton as the Puppy Patrol – thanks to Hasheem.

"No such luck!" Neil grinned. "We were just talking about Mr Grundy."

Hasheem rolled his eyes. "He's not a human being, he's a robot!" he exclaimed. "Have you heard the latest? He wants us to cut down on art lessons, and do more maths and English instead, so he can save money on materials!"

Neil and Chris were outraged.

"Who told you that?" Neil asked.

Hasheem shrugged. "One of the kids overheard him talking to Smiler. It's all over the school!"

"It's just the kind of thing he'd do," Neil agreed, wondering what other ideas Mr Grundy might come up with to save money at Meadowbank Primary . . .

"It's disgusting!" Emily raged. "He can't do it!"

"We've got to stop him, that's for sure," Neil said urgently. "Mr Grundy isn't going to get away with this!"

"What are we going to do then?" Chris asked.

It was the end of the school day, and Neil and Chris had met up with Emily in the playground near the bike sheds. They were still stunned by what had happened at the end of the afternoon, just before the home bell. A letter had been handed to every pupil for their parents. Mr Grundy was "pleased to inform parents that from now on school pets were no longer appropriate". The rabbits, hamsters, guinea-pigs and gerbils which were already in residence would be "disposed of" at the earliest opportunity.

"He should leave our animals alone!" Emily said angrily. "Why on earth does he want to get rid of them?"

"To save money, I suppose," Neil muttered. The decision to get rid of the animals had come as a complete shock to the whole school, and some of the younger children had burst into tears when they were told. Although it was ten minutes since the home bell, there were still some groups of children hanging around outside, discussing this latest development.

"Well, it's not right!" Emily declared passionately. "I bet the other teachers don't like it."

Just at that moment Mr Hamley emerged from the school building staggering under the weight of four carrier bags bulging with exercise books to be marked. Emily charged across the playground towards him, Neil and Chris behind her.

"Mr Hamley!" Emily said breathlessly. "Do *you* think Mr Grundy should take our animals away?"

Mr Hamley frowned. "It's not up to me, I'm afraid, Emily," he said stiffly.

"But the animals are important," Emily went on, regardless. "Some of the children aren't allowed to have pets at home, and keeping them in class is the only chance they get. *And* we get to learn about them, too."

"Well, we're all pretty attached to Tom and Jerry," he admitted reluctantly. Tom and Jerry were the gerbils who belonged to Mr Hamley's class. "But it's Mr Grundy's decision."

"Maybe he'll change his mind when he sees how angry everyone is," Neil suggested.

But Mr Hamley shook his head. "I really can't discuss this," he said shortly. "I'm on my way home, and so should you be."

"I'll be round in a little while to collect Dotty, sir," Neil reminded him.

Mr Hamley nodded and gave a fleeting smile, then hurried off towards the school gates.

"He's much nicer when he's with Dotty," Emily muttered.

"Well, I suppose he feels a bit awkward," Chris said. "He can't very well side with us against Mr Grundy, can he?"

"What are we going to do?" Emily asked, her voice full of despair.

Neil smiled. "I've got an idea," he said triumphantly. "And it's something that's going to make Grumpy Grundy *really* sit up and take notice!"

Chapter Three

"I think a petition is a *brilliant* idea!" Emily said enthusiastically as she, Neil and Sam walked up to the Hamleys' front door. Neil had gone home to collect Sam, and Emily had decided to come with him to walk Dotty. "It's one of the best ideas you've ever had!"

"Thanks," Neil said modestly. "Just call me a genius!"

Emily pulled a face at him. "A show-off, more like! I hope we get loads of signatures!"

"Yeah, that'll show Mr Grundy we mean business and—" Neil broke off hastily as Mr Hamley opened the door. "Hello, sir." Neil had to raise his voice to be heard above the baby

29

screaming inside the house. "Is Dotty ready for her walk?"

Mr Hamley nodded, looking distracted. He disappeared down the hallway, and came back with Dotty bounding alongside him on her lead.

"Hello, girl." Neil patted the Dalmatian as she jumped up at him, wagging her tail furiously.

"Down, Dotty," Mr Hamley snapped. "Don't take her too far, will you? I don't want her tired out." And he shut the door abruptly.

"Well!" Emily exclaimed as they went down the path with the two dogs. "He didn't even say thank you!"

"I think Mr Hamley's got more important things to worry about," Neil said with a grin. "Did you hear the baby? It didn't stop crying the whole time we were there!"

"He did look pretty wound-up," Emily admitted. She giggled as Dotty, who was now trotting alongside Sam, turned and gave the collie's ear a friendly nip. Sam was too well-trained to do the same back, but he wagged his tail hard in response. "Dotty seems happy enough anyway!"

Neil agreed. Then he frowned. "I just hope Mr Hamley realizes what he's taken on. Puppies can be a lot of hard work."

"As long as Dotty doesn't have one hundred and one Dalmatians!" Emily doubled over with laughter at her own joke, and Neil grinned.

"I think we ought to sort out what we're going to do about the petition," he said, as they left Compton behind and walked out into the countryside. "Mr Grundy's a fast worker. He'll have the classroom animals out before we know it."

Emily nodded. "We'd better do it tonight. What should it say?"

"Something like: 'Save our Pets! We want Meadowbank School to keep our classroom animals to help our education'?" Neil suggested. "And then plenty of room for signatures underneath that. We're going to need quite a few copies."

"We'd better get to work as soon as we get in then," Emily said. "Do you think we could get some of the parents to sign it?"

"Yep, I reckon they will!" Neil said, rumpling Sam's coat affectionately before letting him off his lead. Emily let Dotty loose too, and the two dogs trotted off across the field, teasing each other with playful barks. "And we should start with Mum and Dad – Sarah's really upset about it."

Emily smirked. "Mr Grundy's going to be *so* mad when he finds out!"

Neil shrugged. "He's usually in a bad mood anyway, so it won't make much difference."

They stayed in the field for about fifteen minutes exercising the dogs, and Neil kept a close watch on both Dotty and Sam as they chased one another round in circles, enjoying each other's company. It took him a while to persuade Dotty that it was time to go home, but eventually he got her lead on and they all headed back to Mr Hamley's house.

Neil's teacher was looking marginally less stressed when he opened the door. The baby had

stopped screaming, and Mr Hamley had a big mug of tea in his hands. This time he thanked them quite warmly for taking Dotty out, and Neil arranged to call for her again on Wednesday after school. He felt a bit guilty about leaving his dad to run the Kennels single-handed, but he couldn't let Mr Hamley and Dotty down – not with a brood of little Dotties on the way.

"How was the barking mad Dalmatian?" Carole Parker asked, as Neil, Emily and Sam clattered into the kitchen. She was sitting at the table with Sarah, who was drawing a picture, crayons spread out around her.

"She's fine." Neil emptied Sam's bowl, and filled it with fresh water. The collie wagged his tail gratefully, and took a long drink. "Mr Hamley seems more worried than she is!"

"How's your hand, Mum?" Emily asked.

Carole shrugged. "Not too bad. I haven't been able to do anything today, though."

"Never mind," Neil said quickly. "You'll soon be OK again." Carole didn't say anything, but Neil thought she looked a bit anxious. He could guess why his mum was feeling bad, though. With Kate away and Carole out of action, Bob Parker was swamped with work.

"Did you read Mr Grundy's letter about the classroom animals, Mum?" Emily asked. "Don't you think it *stinks*?"

"I think it's horrible," Sarah said huffily. "I know the school pets aren't as clever as Fudge, but why does he want to get rid of them?"

Neil grinned. Fudge was Sarah's hamster, and according to her, he was the most intelligent hamster who had ever lived. No one else in the family had seen any sign of it though.

"He's trying to save the school some money," Neil replied. "But I don't think the animals cost that much to keep anyway."

"Mr Grundy does seem to have a great talent for putting people's backs up," Carole Parker agreed, glancing at the letter again.

"That's why we've started a petition!" Emily told their mother exactly what they were planning, and Carole looked interested. "Well, there's certainly no harm in making your views known," she said. "As long as you go about it properly and peacefully."

"It won't be peaceful with Em about!" Neil said, and Emily stuck her tongue out at him. "Does Dad need a hand, Mum?"

"I'm sure he does." Carole's smile disappeared. "Why don't you go and see?"

Neil checked on Sam, who was already dozing under the kitchen table, then he went over to the kennels.

His father was in Kennel Block One, just coming out of Duke's pen. Neil felt his heart miss a beat as he approached the pen, but Duke was looking subdued, gulping down the food Bob had just given him. Bob had taken sole charge of caring for Duke, and no one else was allowed in the pen.

"Do you want a hand, Dad?"

Duke raised his head at the sound of Neil's voice, and stared miserably at him through the fencing. Neil couldn't help feeling sorry for the dog. "Hello, boy," he said softly, but Duke didn't respond any further. He turned his back on Neil and went through the door that led to the outdoor run.

"That's one miserable dog," Bob Parker remarked, as he unlocked the next pen. "I wish I knew why he's the way he is."

"Do you think it's the Carters' fault?" Neil asked sadly. He hated to see any dog in pain, physical or mental.

"We'll soon find out when they get back on

Saturday morning," Bob said, grimly. "Do you want to feed Buttons for me?"

"Sure!" Neil said, cheering up. Buttons was a friendly little dog, a black and white mongrel, bright-eyed and lively. Although she had found it difficult to settle on her first visit to King Street, she was now completely at home whenever she visited, and she launched herself at Neil, barking a welcome as he went into the pen.

"Good girl!" Neil stroked her, then put the bowl down. Buttons immediately set to and gobbled up the food, her tail still wagging furiously.

"How's Dotty?" Bob asked, as Neil came out of Buttons' pen.

"Fighting fit!" Neil said with a grin.

"That's good news." Bob, who was looking exhausted, yawned and rubbed his eyes. "I'm whacked. I'd really appreciate it if you and Emily could help out with walking the dogs before school tomorrow."

"I'll get up a bit earlier," Neil promised, trying hard to sound enthusiastic. It was important that the dogs' routine was not disturbed, even while the kennels were short-handed, and Neil was determined that the dogs would not suffer.

Anyway, it was only for a few days until his mother and Kate were back at work.

"Ow!" Carole Parker complained, moving her bandaged hand gingerly to and fro. "It still feels painful."

Bob finished off his toast and got up from the breakfast table. "You'd better rest it again today, love. I can manage."

Carole looked upset. "I can still get on with the paperwork . . ." she began.

But Bob shook his head. "Be sensible, Carole. You won't be able to hold a pen properly."

"I can use the computer though," Carole argued, looking determined.

Neil, who was hurriedly bolting down some cereal after taking some of the dogs for a run, wondered why his mother's hand didn't seem to be getting any better. The injury must have been even worse than he'd thought.

"Hurry up, you slowcoaches!" Emily burst into the kitchen, waving a sheaf of papers in one hand. "We've got to get to school early to start collecting signatures for our petition!"

"Ah, yes, the famous petition!" Bob remarked, pulling his coat on. "Are you going to let us sign it?"

"Sure!" Emily said, proudly. "You'll be the first – well, after me and Neil, of course!"

"I want to sign it too!" Sarah insisted.

Emily gave one of the sheets she was holding to her father. She and Neil had spent ages on the computer the previous night making the petition look as professional as possible. The heading was *Save Our Pets!* in big, black letters, and the space for signatures had been neatly divided up into separate boxes for names and addresses.

Bob signed it quickly, then passed the sheet to Carole, who, as he had predicted, found it a real struggle to write. By the time Sarah had laboriously printed out her full name in capital letters, Emily was dancing impatiently from one foot to the other.

"Come *on*, we've got to go!"

Neil quickly said goodbye to Sam, and Bob ushered all of them out of the house and into the Range Rover. Neil crammed his bike into the boot and jumped inside. He didn't usually enjoy arriving at school with his sisters, but today was a special occasion. He and Emily needed to start collecting signatures together.

"Good luck!" their mother called after them.

They arrived at school well before the

morning bell. There were plenty of people around, including a circle of parents at the school gates.

"Did you get the petition drawn up?" Chris asked eagerly, running over to meet them.

Emily nodded, and pulled the pile of papers out of her bag. "We need to get as many signatures as we can before the bell goes," she said urgently.

Chris grinned. "I've already got a queue of people lined up!" He pointed at a small group of pupils from Mr Hamley's class, including Hasheem, who were hanging around by the bike sheds. "They're all waiting to sign!"

Neil, Emily and Chris headed over to them.

"Come on then," said Hasheem cheerfully. "Where's this petition?"

Neil grabbed one of the printed sheets from Emily, and gave it to him.

"I'll ask some of the other kids," Emily decided.

"No need for that," Hasheem said, signing his name with a flourish. He cupped both hands round his mouth and yelled: "If you want to keep your school pets, come and sign our petition! Guaranteed to make Mr Grundy sit up and take notice!"

"Thanks, Hasheem!" Neil said, as kids began to hurry over to see what was going on. "Who needs a loudspeaker system with you around?"

Suddenly everyone in the playground seemed to want to sign the petition. Neil, Emily and Chris were swamped from all sides, and were kept busy handing round the sheets of paper.

"We ought to try and get some parents' signatures too before the bell," Emily muttered to Neil.

"I'll go and ask them." Neil prepared to

shoulder his way out of the mass of children milling round, but it was too late. A tall, ramrod-straight figure was striding towards them, looking very angry indeed.

"Can somebody please tell me what on *earth* is going on here?"

Neil's heart sank. It was Mr Grundy.

Chapter Four

"**W**ell?" Mr Grundy sat behind his dauntingly large desk in his head teacher's office, the crumpled sheets of the petition in front of him. "Would one of you like to explain the meaning of that *disgusting* scene in the playground this morning?"

Neil, Emily and Chris sat on metal chairs in front of the desk and shuddered.

Neil wondered what the head teacher was expecting them to say. After all, it was obvious what they had been doing. "We were collecting signatures, Mr Grundy," he said, "for our petition."

"I can see that!" Mr Grundy snapped. "You

come to school to work, not to get involved in foolish escapades like this," he went on sternly. "I shall be writing to your parents—"

"Our parents signed the petition, sir," Neil pointed out.

Mr Grundy glared at him. "We'll have no more of this nonsense in my school." He picked up the petition, ripped the sheets in half and threw them into the waste-paper basket.

Emily gasped, outraged. "But we just want to keep our animals, sir! No one wants to get rid of them except you—"

"That's enough!" Mr Grundy looked so fierce that Neil couldn't help feeling a little afraid of him. "I expect you to stay in and do extra maths at morning break. I will supervise you personally."

"What a creep!" Emily said indignantly, when they were dismissed. "He didn't even *bother* to listen to what we had to say!"

"All that hard work for nothing!" Chris groaned.

"Never mind," Neil said. "We can easily print off some more sheets."

"But he won't let us collect signatures in school!" Emily wailed, frustrated.

Neil grinned. "OK, so we're not allowed to

collect signatures in *school*. But he can't stop us from doing it *outside*, can he?"

Chris smiled. "Well, it's cheeky, but it might work."

"He'll probably have us arrested!" Emily laughed.

"Well, let's come back tomorrow morning with a new petition and collect signatures outside the school gates," Neil said in a determined voice. "Grumpy Grundy might think he's beaten us, but we're not finished yet!"

"I have a note to read to you from Mr Grundy," Mr Hamley announced to his class just before lunchtime.

Neil nudged Hasheem. "Guess what this is about," he whispered.

Mr Hamley cleared his throat. "*There will be no change in the decision regarding the school animals*," he read out, with a glance at the gerbils' cage in the corner of the classroom. Tom and Jerry were asleep, curled up together in a furry ball, blissfully unaware of their impending fate. "*They will be removed at the end of the week*."

The whole class began to mutter, and Neil

44

frowned. That meant they'd only got three days left to change Grundy's mind. *If* they could change his mind.

"Put your work away, please," called Mr Hamley as the bell for lunchtime rang out. At the same time he hastily put up his hand to smother a yawn, and Neil noticed again how tired he was looking. He couldn't help smiling too as he spotted that Mr Hamley was wearing odd socks, one navy blue and one black. What with the teacher's heavy workload, as well as Dotty and the new baby to cope with, it was no wonder that he seemed distracted.

"Do you really think the petition is going to do any good?" Chris asked as he and Neil met up in the cloakroom and went to lunch. The canteen was a low-roofed but spacious extension, which had been added onto the side of the two-storey school building.

"Not if it's just us lot who are signing it," Neil replied above the din of clattering plates and multiple conversations. "Grumpy won't take any notice of us. But if we can get some of the parents involved . . ."

"Yeah, you're right!" Chris agreed. "This one needs parent power. I bet loads of them are as fed up with Mr Grundy as we are."

Hasheem was already in the queue at the serving-hatch when Neil and Chris joined it. He saw them and made being-sick noises.

"Thanks very much!" Neil said. "I thought you were a mate!"

"Not you – the food!" Hasheem groaned. "Haven't you seen it? It's gross!"

Neil and Chris stood on tiptoe and stared over the heads of the people in front of them. They could see a pie that looked rock-hard, some lumpy mashed potato and a large, watery bowl of grey stuff.

"That's disgusting!" Chris said, pulling a face. "That grey thing looks like a chemical experiment!"

Neil wondered what had happened. Their school dinners were usually quite good, although they weren't always very exciting.

"Mince or cheese and onion pie?" asked the dinner-lady, as the three boys reached the serving-hatch.

"Oh, thanks for letting us know what they are," Hasheem said. "It's kind of impossible to tell."

"We'll have less of your cheek, thank you, Hasheem Lindon!" said the dinner-lady, but only half-heartedly.

46

"What happened to the food?" Hasheem went on. "You know, the stuff we could actually eat?"

"We've changed to a different caterer," the dinner-lady said shortly, picking up a serving-spoon.

"Mr Grundy!" Neil hissed at the others. "I bet he's changed the caterers to save money!"

The boys took their plates over to an empty table and sat down.

"Mind your teeth on the cheese and onion pie!" Neil advised the others, once he'd managed to saw through the pastry.

Hasheem took a taste of the mashed potato, and almost spat it out again.

"More lumps than mash!" he spluttered.

"Grundy's done it again," Neil sighed. "Everyone at Meadowbank Primary is going to be up in arms over this."

When afternoon lessons began again after lunch, some of the children in Neil's class complained to Mr Hamley about the school dinners. Neil didn't, because he felt sorry for the exhausted teacher. But all through the afternoon he couldn't help feeling that a dark cloud of resentment was hanging over the school because everyone was fed up with Mr Grundy's behaviour. It really depressed Neil. Meadowbank Primary had always been such a happy school, and he'd enjoyed going there – well, as much as anyone could enjoy school, anyway. Now he was relieved when the bell rang and he could go home.

"Don't forget to bring some more petition sheets tomorrow!" Chris called after Neil as he cycled off towards his house.

Neil waved, and headed off on his own bike towards King Street Kennels, where Sam rushed to meet him. Neil knelt down and made a huge fuss of the collie, reassuring Sam, as he always did, that he'd missed him enormously while he was at school.

48

His mother was in the kitchen, and she looked up as Neil came in. "Hi, how was your day?"

"Mr Grundy ripped up our petition, and our school dinners were disgusting," Neil replied. "Apart from that, it was great."

Carole looked sympathetic as Neil explained exactly what had happened. "I think Mr Grundy's going a bit too far," she remarked. "But he *is* new. Maybe he'll calm down soon."

Neil wasn't very hopeful. "Are you feeling better, Mum?" he asked, looking at her bandaged hand.

Carole shrugged. "I'm all right. Your dad's gone to pick up the girls, and then he's going to buy some supplies."

Neil couldn't help noticing that she changed the subject rather quickly. "For the dogs?" he asked.

"No, for us!" Carole grinned ruefully. "I haven't been able to go shopping."

"OK, I'll make a start on walking the dogs before Dad gets back," Neil offered. "I was hoping I might have time to go and see Jake tonight, though." Neil couldn't wait for Jake to move to King Street Kennels, and he loved visiting the perky pup at Old Mill Farm.

"That shouldn't be a problem," his mother said.

"Great!" Neil knelt down and put his arm round Sam's neck. "Do you want to go and see Jake, boy?"

Sam's bright, alert eyes lit up even more, and he gave a short, sharp bark.

"I think that means yes!" Neil grinned. "Are you ready for a walk then, Sam?"

Sam barked again, and looked around for his lead. He spotted it hanging over a chair, and went to retrieve it.

"Why don't you come with us, Mum?" Neil suggested. "Some fresh air might do you good."

"No, I don't think so," Carole said quickly.

"Oh, go on, Mum," Neil urged her. "We'll take Buttons and Robbie; they love going for walks with Sam." Robbie was a golden Labrador who was on his first visit to the kennels while his owner was in hospital.

Carole was shaking her head even before Neil had finished speaking. "I said no, Neil," she snapped. "Now get a move on, if you're going."

Neil didn't say anything else. He and Sam went out of the house and over to Kennel Block One to collect the dogs, but all the time Neil was thinking hard. There was definitely something wrong with his mother, and it wasn't just the injury to her hand. She had over-reacted badly to his suggestion that she come with him to walk the dogs. At the moment Carole didn't seem like the calm, capable woman Neil knew, and he suspected that she hadn't been back to the kennel blocks since Duke had bitten her.

A sudden thought hit him hard, and he stopped, dismayed, to consider the implications. Had his mother lost her nerve with the dogs?

Chapter Five

"**M**um?" Neil had hung around deliberately after breakfast the next day to have a quiet word with his mother, refusing a lift to school from his father who had gone off earlier with Emily and Sarah. Emily hadn't been too pleased because they were supposed to be collecting signatures for the petition again that morning. But Neil felt he had to do something right away, if his suspicions about his mother were true. He had slept badly the night before, wondering if he was right, and, if he was, what that would mean for King Street Kennels.

"You'd better hurry or you'll be late," Carole remarked, as she cleared the breakfast table.

It seemed to Neil that she was avoiding his eye. "Mum, about what happened with Duke," he began in a determined voice.

"That's over and done with." Carole turned away from Neil so that he couldn't see her face, but he was sure that he was right. His mother *had* lost her nerve with the dogs.

Neil wondered if the injury to her hand was still as bad as she claimed, or if she was pretending it was still painful to avoid the kennels. "All right, so when are you going to start helping out with the dogs again?"

His mother took a deep breath before replying. "When my hand's a little better, Neil. Anyway, Kate should be back on Monday, and then things will get easier."

"They say if you fall off a horse, you should get straight back on again," Neil pointed out, his heart hammering with anxiety. He hated seeing his mother like this, but it made him realize just how much the attack had affected her.

"What do you mean?" Carole asked in a threatening tone.

Neil knew he ought to stop right there, but he couldn't. "Well, if the dogs are making you nervous now, you ought to start going into the kennels again."

Carole Parker controlled herself with a visible effort. "Neil, I'm fine, and I'll be back at work before you know it."

"Maybe if you talked to Dad—" Neil began.

"No," Carole said sharply. "And I don't want you bothering him either. He's got quite enough on his plate at the moment."

"But—"

"I mean it, Neil."

He nodded reluctantly. He never argued with his mother when she spoke to him in that particular tone.

Neil went slowly out of the house. Well, he'd made a right mess of that, hadn't he? He climbed onto his bike and pedalled off towards Compton, wondering what was going to happen next. His mother had always been completely involved in the kennels, and she loved dogs as much as his father did. Neil didn't want to think about what the consequences would be if Carole decided she didn't want to work with dogs any more.

"Hey, Neil!" Chris was cycling furiously to meet him. "I thought we were supposed to get to school early to collect signatures? You're going about as fast as a snail with a limp!"

Neil blinked. He'd been so worried about his

mum, he'd almost forgotten about the petition. "Sorry!"

The two boys raced to the school. By the time they got there, Emily was already surrounded by a huge crowd of children and parents outside the school gates, all busily signing the new petition.

"About time too!" Emily snapped when Neil and Chris arrived. "I'm drowning in signatures!"

The two boys grabbed some sheets of paper, and joined in. There was even more interest today than there had been before. Word had got round that the head teacher had ripped up the first petition, and now everyone was even more indignant.

"I really think Mr Grundy should change his mind about this," said Mrs Jones, as she signed her name. Her daughter, Kathy, was in Neil's class.

"Maybe the PTA could make a formal protest," another mother suggested.

"Or we could complain to the chairman of the governors, that nice Mr Bingham," said another.

Neil, Emily and Chris shot each other delighted looks. This time Mr Grundy wouldn't be able to ignore their petition, Neil thought triumphantly. Then his heart began to race as he looked up and saw the head teacher hurrying across the playground towards them. Mr Grundy looked as if he was ready to explode with fury.

"Quick, collect up all the sheets!" Neil said under his breath. They just about managed to get all them back before Mr Grundy reached the gate, and Emily flicked through them, counting under her breath.

"We've filled nearly eleven pages!" she whispered to Neil and Chris.

Neil did a quick calculation. There was room for ten signatures on each page which meant

they had collected over one hundred signatures! That thought gave Neil the courage to stand up straight and meet Mr Grundy's accusing glare.

"What is going on out here?" he asked tightly. "Didn't you hear the bell?"

"Here, sir." Neil took the sheets from Emily, and handed them over to the head teacher. "We'd really like to keep the animals in our classrooms, and so would everyone who's signed our petition."

Mr Grundy stared down at the sheets of paper as if he'd like to shred them into bits right there and then. But as Neil had guessed, he didn't dare while there were parents standing round watching.

"Well," he blustered, "we'll have to see about that."

"I hope you'll reconsider, Mr Grundy," Mrs Jones said. Some of the other parents murmured agreement. "My Kathy's really upset about it."

"I'll certainly . . . take into consideration your . . . heartfelt views," Mr Grundy said coldly. "Now please make your way into school, all of you."

"We did it!" Emily whispered to Neil and Chris, as the head teacher strode off.

Neil shook his head. "Not quite. He hasn't changed his mind yet."

"He will!" Emily said confidently. "You wait and see!"

Chris gave Neil a thumbs-up sign as they went into their separate classrooms. "I reckon we've really made Grumpy sit up and take notice this time!"

Neil nodded, but as he went in to Mr Hamley's classroom, he felt slightly uneasy. He couldn't help wondering what Mr Grundy's next move would be.

"Hurry up, Neil," Mr Hamley snapped. He was already at his desk, register open. "We haven't got all day."

Neil glanced at the teacher as he hurried over to his seat. Mr Hamley looked worse than ever. His shirt hadn't been properly ironed, and he was yawning almost continuously as he took the register. Neil wondered if the teacher was getting any sleep at all. It certainly didn't look like it.

Neil couldn't help worrying about Dotty. He knew how much the Hamleys loved the Dalmatian, but they had such a lot on their plate at the moment. He was concerned that Dotty wasn't getting the special care that a mum-to-be needed.

Still, he would be able to check on the dog

himself when he went round to walk her again after school.

Nobody saw Mr Grundy all that day, and nothing was heard about the petition. But when the home bell rang that afternoon, Mr Hamley handed out yet another letter from the head teacher for the class to take home to their parents. Neil wondered if Mr Grundy had made a final decision about the fate of the school animals, but the letter turned out to be about something quite different.

"*I am very concerned about the standards of dress in our school,*" Neil read aloud as he and Chris walked out into the playground. "*Many of the pupils are letting the school down by not making sure their uniforms are clean and tidy.*"

"*I will therefore be making weekly inspections to check that the pupils' hairstyles, clothes and shoes are of an acceptable standard,*" Chris went on, sounding as pompous as old Grumpy Grundy himself. "*As part of this drive to raise standards, girls will not be permitted to wear trousers to school from next term.*"

Neil raised his eyebrows. "Well, *that's* going to please Em," he began, and right at that moment Emily raced over to them, waving the letter.

"Have you *seen* this?"

Neil and Chris nodded.

"He can't do it!" Emily stormed. "It's against the law – at least, I think it is!"

"I don't think that'll bother Grumpy," Neil remarked. "He does what he likes!"

"We've got to *do* something!" Emily went on determinedly. "I think we should start another petition!"

"Hey, one petition at a time!" Neil said. "Let's sort out the school animals first."

"I'm going to tell Dad!" Emily raged, as she saw their father's Range Rover pull up outside the school gates. "Mr Grundy's got no right to do this!"

"Remind Dad that I'm going to walk Dotty, will you?" Neil shouted after her. "I'll get home as soon as I can."

He said goodbye to Chris and cycled off to Mr Hamley's house. Life was pretty hectic at the moment, Neil thought as he wheeled his bike up the Hamleys' path. In all the excitement about the petition and his concerns about Dotty and his mum, he'd almost forgotten that Duke's owners were returning on Saturday to pick up their dog. Neil wasn't looking forward to that at all.

He leaned his bike against the porch and rang the bell. There was no answer, although Neil could hear Dotty barking somewhere in the house. He wondered where Mr Hamley had got to. If the teacher had had to stay on at school, surely he would have said so? Or maybe Mr Hamley had forgotten their arrangement, Neil thought, dismayed.

"Oh, Neil, sorry to keep you waiting." Mr Hamley hurried up the path towards him, laden down with bags of books and papers. He fumbled for his key and pushed open the door. "Come in."

Neil blinked at the mess in the hallway in front of him. There were all sorts of things strewn around; babies' toys, dog biscuits and newspapers, amongst others. Meanwhile, Dotty could be heard scrabbling frantically at the kitchen door and whining.

"I've had to shut Dotty in the kitchen." Mr Hamley dropped his bags and hurried down the hallway. "Sorry about the mess," he apologized stiffly. "My wife had to go up to Scotland on Monday night. Her mother's been taken ill. I had to rush home at lunchtime to let Dotty out so that she could relieve herself."

"Oh, I'm sorry." Neil began to feel even more alarmed as he realized that Dotty had been left on her own all day. He knew that puppies could arrive up to five days early, and even though Dotty had just over a week to wait before the birth, something could still go wrong. Neil bit his lip. He knew he had to be careful because Mr Hamley was his teacher, but he had to say *something*.

"Mr Hamley," he began, but he didn't have time for anything more. The teacher opened the kitchen door, and Dotty shot out like a rocket, barking loudly. She threw herself at her owner, and then dashed up to Neil, her brown eyes dancing with pleasure.

"Dotty, behave yourself!" Mr Hamley gasped, grabbing the excited dog by her collar. Then he stiffened. "What's that yellow stuff round her mouth?"

Neil looked more closely. Now he could see that Dotty did indeed have bright yellow marks around her jaws.

"D'you think she's got some kind of illness?" Mr Hamley stared at Neil anxiously.

Neil looked again. "No, I don't think she's ill," he said, trying hard not to laugh. "Have you given her any curry recently?"

Mr Hamley suddenly looked guilty. He hurried into the kitchen and Neil and Dotty followed him. The kitchen was a mess too. On the floor were a couple of foil take-away containers which were licked clean.

"I had a take-away curry for dinner last night and I didn't get round to cleaning up," Mr Hamley muttered. "You're a bad girl, Dotty!"

Neil frowned. He wasn't finding the situation very funny now at all. The curry probably wouldn't hurt Dotty, but what if she had eaten something else which *might* have affected her? And anyway, in Dotty's present condition, she certainly shouldn't be left on her own.

"Mr Hamley, is there anyone who can look after Dotty in the daytime?" he asked tentatively. "She really shouldn't be on her own right now."

"I'm quite aware of that, thank you, Neil," Mr Hamley snapped, turning red. "You can rest assured that I've made other arrangements as from tomorrow."

Neil couldn't help wondering what those arrangements were, as he fastened Dotty's lead to her collar. He sighed inwardly as the Dalmatian licked his hand, and looked trustingly up into his face. Neil just hoped that Mr Hamley knew what he was doing, because if he didn't, Dotty would be the one to suffer.

Chapter Six

Whe Neil arrived back at King Street, his mother was in the office. She was at the computer, typing with her good hand, and on the floor was a wire basket with a small, black dog inside. The dog was long-haired, and looked like a woolly teddy-bear. He was shivering and whining piteously, his large, brown eyes fixed on Carole's face, but she wasn't taking much notice of him.

"Hey, who's this?" Neil asked, bending over the basket. The dog instantly shrank back into a corner, looking scared, so Neil let him sniff his hand. When the dog's tail began to wag cautiously, he scratched the top of his shaggy head. "Hello, boy!"

"Sergeant Moorhead brought him in," his mother replied. "He was found wandering round Compton town centre. Nobody claimed him."

"Poor thing." Neil put the basket on the desk, close to where his mother was sitting. She didn't flinch, but she didn't look at the little dog either. Neil felt very depressed. He'd never seen his mother look so uninterested in a dog before, especially a stray. The little dog had begun to whine again as he stared hopefully up at Carole, obviously longing for some attention. "Is he going into the rescue centre?"

Carole nodded. "I'm just adding his details to our records now. Do you want to give him a name?"

"How about Star?" Neil suggested. "He's sure to be a hit with anybody looking for a new puppy."

"OK."

"Star can't have been a stray for very long," Neil said thoughtfully, looking the dog over. "He's been well cared for."

Carole glanced at the dog, and her face softened. "He's a funny little scrap, isn't he? Maybe he's just lost, and his owner will claim him soon. We'd better have Mike in to check him over, though." Mike Turner was the local vet. "Take Star over to the rescue centre, will you, Neil? Your father and Emily are preparing a pen."

"All right," Neil said, picking Star up. He wished his mother had shown the dog a little more attention, but at least she'd seemed touched by the dog's plight. That was a start.

Sam was asleep in his favourite place under the hedge at the bottom of the garden, but he shook himself awake, and raced up to Neil, barking a greeting. At the same time Bob, Emily and Sarah came out of the rescue centre.

"Quiet, Sam!" Neil ordered, as he saw that Star was looking agitated again. "Sit!"

Sam immediately stopped barking, and dropped onto his haunches. Neil then lowered the basket, and let Star and the collie sniff each other cautiously.

"Isn't he *gorgeous*?" Emily called. "I saw him when Sergeant Moorhead brought him in."

"I've called him Star," Neil told her. "Is there a pen ready for him, Dad?"

Bob nodded, and hurried off towards Kennel Block One, Sarah at his heels. Neil noticed how tired his father was looking, and wondered yet again if he ought to talk to him about Carole. He turned to Emily.

"Have you noticed anything strange about Mum?"

"Strange?" Emily looked puzzled. "What do you mean?"

Neil quickly explained, and Emily's eyes widened.

"But Mum loves dogs!" she exclaimed, shocked.

"I know. And maybe she'll get over it soon . . ." Neil tried to sound as if he believed it himself. "She told me not to talk to Dad about it, but I was wondering if I should."

Emily frowned. "He's really busy at the moment. Maybe you should wait a few days until Kate gets back next week. That'll give Mum a bit of time to get more . . . normal."

"Yes, you're probably right."

Star began whining again as Neil carried him into the rescue centre and he scented the presence of other dogs. There were only two other strays at the moment, a Jack Russell called Rufus and a yappy brown mongrel called Lily, and both of them hurried over to take a look at the new arrival.

Neil took Star into an empty pen. He opened up the basket, but the little dog was so nervous, he refused to come out at first. Then, at last, he

stepped out very cautiously, and sniffed his way all round the pen. That didn't seem to reassure him much though, because he then slumped down in a corner, still looking miserable.

"Poor old Star," Neil said sympathetically, ruffling the dog's silky ears. He seemed a nervous animal anyway, and if he had been accidentally separated from his owner, he must have gone through a very traumatic experience. It was a pity his mother hadn't shown the dog more interest, Neil thought, frustrated, because Star had obviously taken a shine to Carole. Maybe a gentle, timid dog like Star was the way to rebuild Carole's confidence in dogs.

Looking down at the sweet-natured,

frightened little dog, Neil had an idea about how to help his mum. He locked Star's pen up, and raced back to the house. Bob and Emily were now cleaning out Kennel Block Two, with Sarah getting under their feet, and Carole was still in the office, so Neil was able to collect what he needed without being seen. Then he hurried straight back to Star.

"Good boy!" he said soothingly as he went into the pen. "Look what I've got for you."

Neil had sneaked into his parents' bedroom, and picked up a favourite sweatshirt of his mother's. He held it out to Star. The dog sniffed it, then began to whine and paw at it. Neil let Star smell the sweatshirt for a few more seconds, then he pulled a small piece of chicken he had snaffled from the fridge out of his pocket, and gave it to the dog. Star gobbled it down eagerly.

"Good boy," Neil said again. He didn't know if his plan would work. He was hoping that Star would associate his mother's scent with the particularly tasty treat and be even more friendly towards her, maybe even encouraging her to go into the pen. It was a bit of a long shot, Neil knew, but he had to try something.

*

Next morning Neil and Emily hurried out before anyone else was up, and went through exactly the same routine several times with Star. Neil had told his sister about his plan, and she was eager to see for herself whether it would work or not. Star had already caught on to this new game, and was waiting hopefully for his treats as soon as he recognized the scent of the sweatshirt.

"Good dog!" Neil said, feeling very pleased as he stroked Star's shaggy little body.

"He's clever, isn't he?" Emily remarked, holding out her hand for Star to lick. "But how are you going to get Mum to come and see him if she's avoiding the dogs?"

"I'm working on it," Neil said.

After breakfast it was time for school, and Neil cycled off to meet Chris as usual.

"D'you think Mr Grundy will tell us what he's decided about the school pets today?" Chris asked, as they rode into Compton.

Neil frowned. "I don't know. Emily's convinced he's going to back down, but I just can't see Grumpy giving in so easily. I wouldn't be surprised if we turned up one morning and all the pets were gone! That's exactly how Grumpy operates."

"Maybe we ought to start a petition to get rid of *him*!" Chris suggested as they went into the playground.

"Well, we'd probably get *thousands* of signatures if we did!" Neil said with a grin.

As the two boys locked up their bikes, Mr Hamley hurried through the school gates, laden down with bags, as usual.

"Smiler's late, isn't he?" Chris remarked. "He's usually here much earlier than this."

Neil didn't say anything. He suspected that the teacher wasn't coping very well with his wife away, but he didn't want to broadcast Mr Hamley's problems around the school. He just hoped that Mr Hamley had got Dotty properly settled in, wherever he had left her.

The bell rang out and Mr Hamley broke into an awkward run, impeded by the heavy bags he was carrying. Suddenly the handle of one of the carriers broke, and books and folders spilled out onto the ground. Neil and Chris immediately dashed over to help.

"Thanks, boys," Mr Hamley said gratefully as they helped him collect his belongings. Neil also retrieved a tin of dog food, which Mr Hamley snatched from him and stuffed into one of the other bags. He looked rather embarrassed, Neil thought curiously. But why? Maybe he didn't want them to know that he was late because he'd been shopping before school. From Mr Hamley's tense expression, Neil thought it was probably wisest to keep quiet, so he walked straight to class in silence.

"Hey!" Hasheem nudged Neil as Mr Hamley's pupils settled themselves down, ready for the register. "What's up with old Smiler today? He looks like he's got ants in his pants!"

Neil glanced over at the teacher. Mr Hamley did look rather jumpy. He was pacing up and down in front of the blackboard, looking as if his mind was miles away. Neil felt rather sorry for him, because he guessed the teacher must be worrying about Dotty, wherever she was.

All through the first half of the morning Mr Hamley seemed on edge. As soon as the bell for break rang, he shot to his feet and called impatiently: "Come on, hurry up and go outside, please."

Neil was still putting his maths books away, when he happened to glance across the classroom at the teacher. He was astonished to see Mr Hamley look round furtively, then slip the tin of dog food into his jacket pocket.

Neil's eyes almost popped out of his head, as

Mr Hamley went briskly out of the classroom. He hurried after him, bumping into Chris who was outside in the corridor.

"Oi!" Chris complained jokingly. "What's the rush?"

"Mr Hamley's just put that tin of dog food in his pocket!" Neil gasped.

"So?" Chris looked puzzled.

Neil didn't wait to explain further. He rushed after Mr Hamley, dragging his friend with him. The teacher was heading for the stairs which led down to the ground floor of the school. They trailed Mr Hamley down the corridor, past a couple of classrooms, including Emily's, and then past the gym.

"You realize we're going to get into big trouble if we're spotted," Chris complained, as they cautiously followed the teacher round a corner. "We're not allowed down this end of the school."

"I know," Neil said. "But something's going on, and I think I know what . . ."

"Stalking a teacher is probably forbidden too," Chris mumbled on.

Neil grabbed Chris's arm and they ducked out of sight behind a cupboard as Mr Hamley stopped and went inside a room right at the end of the long corridor, closing the door quietly behind him.

"That's the boiler room!" Neil muttered.

"So what?" Chris said. "Maybe Mr Hamley wants a word with Mr Johnson." Mr Johnson was the caretaker at Meadowbank Primary.

Neil shook his head. "I don't think so." He tiptoed over to the door, with Chris behind him, and then stopped.

Suddenly the door was opened again before either of the boys had a chance to flee. Mr Hamley was standing there, glaring at them. "What are you two doing here?" he demanded furiously. "You know very well it's out of bounds, and—"

He didn't have a chance to say any more. The very next second Dotty raced joyfully out of the room behind him, and flung herself at Neil, barking a welcome.

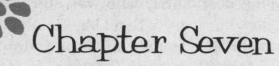

Chapter Seven

"Dotty!" Mr Hamley turned bright red, and made a futile grab at the Dalmatian's collar. Dotty dodged him, still barking, and dashed from Neil to Chris, jumping up at them in turn, her tail thrashing wildly from side to side.

"Dotty, be quiet!" Mr Hamley gasped. He grabbed at the Dalmatian again, and this time he managed to control her. He pulled Dotty back into the room, and Neil and Chris followed. It was warm and cosy in there because of the large boiler in one corner and the heating pipes running along the walls. Dotty's dog basket lay on the floor with a bowl of water next to it, and a selection of rubber toys.

Neil glanced at Chris, who was still looking amazed. So *this* was where Mr Hamley was keeping Dotty! The teacher must have dropped her off early this morning before anyone else was around, then gone back home to collect his books. That explained why he was late.

"What are you two doing down here?" Mr Hamley snapped, trying to sound authoritative as Dotty stared at them, her eyes bright with mischief. "You know this area is out of bounds!"

"Sorry, sir," said Neil and Chris together.

Mr Hamley sighed. "I might have known I couldn't keep Dotty a secret. Oh, well, it was worth a try."

"Won't the caretaker find out anyway?" Neil asked.

"Mr Johnson's been – er – helping me out," Mr Hamley confessed. "He knows Dotty's here, and he's been checking up on her while I'm teaching. But he's the only one who knows."

Meaning that Mr Grundy didn't, Neil thought. "We won't tell anyone, sir," he said eagerly. "We could help you too."

Mr Hamley looked embarrassed again. "No, that wouldn't be right," he said shortly. "I'll just have to make other arrangements." He sighed. "The trouble is, there isn't really anywhere else

I can leave Dotty, and my wife won't be back till next week."

"It really is better if Dotty stays with you, sir," Neil pointed out gently. "Moving her around too much will upset her."

Mr Hamley cleared his throat as the bell for the end of break rang in the distance. "Yes, I can see that, Neil. Now off you go back to class."

Neil and Chris gave Dotty a final pat, and then hurried out of the room.

"You guessed Dotty was in there, didn't you?" Chris whispered to Neil as they went back towards their classrooms.

"Mr Hamley putting that tin of dog food in his pocket kind of gave it away!" Neil grinned.

"D'you think he'll carry on keeping Dotty there?"

Neil shrugged. "For the moment. He doesn't seem to have much choice, and her puppies aren't due for another week or so. Dotty ought to be at home for the birth though. She might be unsettled if she's in a strange place."

"Let's hope Mr Grundy doesn't find out. If he doesn't want hamsters and gerbils in school, he's not going to want a dog!"

"I know." Neil looked worried. If the head teacher found out what was going on, Mr

Hamley would be in serious trouble. He hoped that Dotty would behave herself while she was hidden and not give their secret away, but, of course, no one ever knew quite what Dotty would do next . . .

Neil found it difficult to concentrate on his work for the rest of the day. He was on edge all the time, and he kept stopping every few minutes to listen for the sound of Dotty barking. The boiler room was right underneath Mr Hamley's classroom, but Neil couldn't hear a thing. Dotty was probably asleep for most of the day anyway, so it looked like her hiding-place would remain undiscovered, at least for the next few days.

As the home bell rang, Neil wondered how Mr Hamley was going to get Dotty out of the school again. Presumably the teacher would have to wait until everyone else had gone home before he smuggled her out. Neil wished there was something he could do to help, but he didn't want to push it. Mr Hamley was obviously embarrassed enough at being caught out by two pupils.

"I got told off about a million times by Mrs Stewart!" Chris confessed as he and Neil cycled home. "I just couldn't concentrate because I was thinking about Dotty."

"Me too," Neil agreed. "I just hope Smiler gets her out of school safely tonight. It'd be just his luck to run slap-bang into Mr Grundy!"

"Talking of Grundy," Chris went on, "isn't it about time he told us what he's going to do about the school animals? He's had nearly all week to think it over."

"Maybe he'll tell us tomorrow. It's Friday and I'll bet he'll want it sorted by the weekend."

"Or maybe he thinks if he keeps quiet, we'll forget about it," Chris suggested.

"With Em around? No chance!" Neil laughed. "See you tomorrow."

When Neil arrived home, no one was around except Sam, who jumped up to greet him, and his mother, who was again in the office at the computer.

She was typing swiftly with both hands, but stopped abruptly as Neil walked in. "Hello, love. Had a good day?"

"OK." Neil had already decided not to say anything at home about Dotty being kept at school. It was Mr Hamley's secret, not his. "How's Star?"

"Your father said he seems better today."

Carole began to type again, but one-handed this time.

Neil's heart sank. His mother's hand was obviously getting better, even if she didn't want to admit it. How much longer could she keep this up?

"Mike should be here soon to check him over," she went on.

"I'll go and see Star now," Neil decided. "D'you want to come with me, Mum?"

Carole shook her head. "I want to get this paperwork finished."

Neil didn't argue, because he knew it wouldn't do any good. He popped into the house, collected his mother's sweatshirt from upstairs and some chunky ham slices from the fridge and went to Star's pen.

The little dog was asleep, but he uncurled himself and rushed across the pen on his short, stumpy legs, tail going from side to side.

"Here, boy!" Neil murmured, holding out the sweatshirt. Star sniffed at it, and then barked expectantly, his eyes locking on to the ham in Neil's hand. Neil handed it over, and Star gulped it down.

"Good dog!" Neil scratched Star's woolly coat, pleased that his plan was working so well, although it wouldn't be any use unless he could bring Star and his mother together. That was going to be difficult, unless somehow he could get his mother over to the rescue centre . . .

"Hi, Neil!" Mike Turner walked into the rescue centre, carrying his medical bag. He was often called in at the kennels, and knew the Parker family very well. "How's the new arrival?"

"He's a brilliant little dog," Neil said, as Mike let himself into the pen. "He was a bit nervous yesterday, but he's calmed down now."

"I'd better let *him* check *me* out first, then!" Mike waited patiently for Star to sniff at him cautiously, then knelt down to look him over. Star submitted patiently to the examination. "He's been very well cared for," he said, at last. "That shaggy coat of his would be a lot more tangled if he'd been a stray for any length of time."

"We're hoping his owners are looking for him," Neil began, then he broke off as his mother appeared unexpectedly in the doorway.

"Mike?" Carole's voice sounded a little wobbly to Neil as she walked into the rescue centre. "Janice just phoned." Janice was Mike's receptionist at the surgery. "Your mobile is switched off. She said could you go on to Longbrook Farm when you've finished here, as there's a problem with one of the cows."

"Thanks, Carole." Mike smiled at her, then glanced at Star. "Hey, boy, what on *earth's* the matter with you?"

Star had scented Carole Parker now and had pulled away from the vet. He raced up to the wire fence and pawed at it, whining loudly, his brown eyes shining underneath his curtain of long hair.

"I think you've got an admirer, Carole!" Mike said teasingly, and Neil was thrilled to see that his mother couldn't help smiling. She glanced down at the excited dog, and Neil held his breath. Then very slowly Carole bent down and put her good hand to the wire fence. Star strained to lick her fingers, and although Carole flinched slightly, Neil was thrilled to see that she didn't pull away. Then she stroked the dog's head, and Star looked up at her adoringly.

"I'd better get over to the farm, then," Mike said.

Neil was feeling very proud of himself, as Carole gave Star another pat, and then followed Mike out. His plan was working! He was becoming increasingly hopeful now that, with Star's

help, his mother would soon be back to normal.

Bob and the girls arrived home just as Mike was leaving.

"Where've you been – Timbuctoo?" Neil remarked. "I got home ages ago!"

Emily rolled her eyes. "Sarah forgot her reading book and we had to turn round and go back to school to get it!"

"*Sor-ree!*" Sarah said with dignity. "I'm trying

to teach Fudge to read, and that's the book we're up to!"

"Talking of hamsters," Mike remarked, "I'll be coming to your school tomorrow to pick up the pets."

Neil and Emily stared at him.

"*What*?" Emily gasped.

Mike looked puzzled. "I thought you all knew. Your head teacher phoned me this afternoon, and asked me if I could – well – 'dispose of them' are actually the words he used."

"The horrible creep!" Emily burst out. "He didn't even tell us what he was planning!"

"I suppose he was just going to have the animals taken away, and not tell us till it was all over!" Neil exclaimed angrily. "Typical Grumpy!"

Mike frowned. "I persuaded him to let me try and re-home them. But I didn't realize he was going ahead behind everyone's back."

"It's not your fault, Mike," Bob pointed out.

"Well, the whole thing does seem unfair on the kids – I know they've put a lot of work into looking after those animals," Mike said grimly.

As the vet went out, Neil turned to Emily. "Well, that's that then," he said gloomily. "Mr Grundy's got the better of us once and for all."

"Not quite!" Emily retorted. She marched

over to the telephone, a determined look on her face. "I think it's time we let Jake Fielding at the *Compton News* know about this!"

"So Emily rang the *Compton News* last night and spoke to Jake Fielding, and he's coming over to do a story about the school animals this morning!" Neil told Chris triumphantly as they cycled into the playground. Jake Fielding, a young photographer with the local newspaper, had covered stories at King Street Kennels several times. "That'll show Mr Grundy we mean business!"

"Good one!" Chris said, pleased. "I can't believe Grumpy was just going to get rid of the animals!"

Neil shrugged. "That's what Grundy's like, though, isn't it? I mean, he really doesn't care what we think."

Hasheem caught the end of Neil's sentence and grinned. "What's he done now?"

"Wait till you hear this!" Neil said.

The news about Mr Grundy was all over the school in no time. Everyone was disgusted about his plans, and by the time Neil got to his classroom several of his friends were already complaining loudly to Mr Hamley. The teacher was looking a bit distracted.

"Ah, Neil." Mr Hamley hurried over as soon as

he saw him. "I – er – brought Dotty in early this morning and I haven't had a chance to check up on her since," he said in a low voice. "So I was wondering . . ."

"Do you want me to go and see her?" Neil asked in an undertone.

Mr Hamley nodded gratefully, and Neil quietly slipped out of the classroom. There was no one around as he hurried down to the boiler room. When he pulled the door open, Dotty, who was curled up in her basket looking sleepy, immediately leaped out to meet him.

"Hello, Spotty Dotty!" Neil whispered, stroking the dog's soft, gleaming coat. Dotty snuggled lovingly up against him, but Neil didn't dare stay too long. He gave Dotty a final caress, then went over to the door.

Dotty followed him.

"No, Dotty!" Neil said sternly. "Basket!"

Dotty whined, looking crestfallen, but she climbed in and curled up again. Neil suddenly heard footsteps and quickly left the room.

"What are you doing in there, Neil Parker!"

The loud, accusing voice from the other end of the corridor made Neil almost jump out of his skin. He turned to see Mr Grundy advancing furiously towards him.

"Mr Hamley sent me to look for the caretaker, sir." Neil prayed desperately that Dotty wouldn't start barking at the sound of his voice. "There's something wrong with the radiator in our classroom."

"I see." Mr Grundy looked marginally less angry. "I'm looking for Mr Johnson myself. Is he in there?" And the head teacher gestured towards the boiler room.

"No, sir," Neil answered, his heart thumping so loudly, he was sure Grumpy must be able to hear it.

"Well, go straight back to class please," said Mr Grundy shortly, and he went off down the corridor.

Shaking with relief, Neil hurried back upstairs to the classroom. That had been too close a shave for his liking.

"Was everything all right, Neil?" Mr Hamley asked as the class lined up for assembly. Neil nodded. He didn't see any point in worrying the teacher even further by telling him what had happened. He joined the end of the line, and followed the rest of his class into the hall.

The hall was large, but with the whole school in there, sitting in rows on the floor, there was hardly any space to move. Mr Grundy was already in there, pacing up and down on the low platform which stood at one end of the room. Neil's class was last to go in, and the head teacher glared at them for keeping him waiting.

"Before we start our assembly," Mr Grundy began loudly, staring down at the rows of children seated in front of him, "I wish to clear up the matter of the school animals."

Neil turned round to glance at Chris. Obviously the head teacher had been forced into this announcement because he'd been found out. Neil was sure that Grumpy had planned to move the animals secretly, so that the pupils wouldn't have a chance to complain any further.

"The pets will be removed later today, and re-homed," Mr Grundy went on, speaking even more loudly as some people began to mutter and complain to one another. "Silence, please, and let me finish! Whatever some of you may think, a school is no place to keep animals!"

Suddenly the sound of a dog barking could be heard, and a chill came over Neil. Next second a very excited, heavily pregnant Dalmatian romped joyfully through the open doors into the hall, barking madly and looking very pleased with herself indeed. Dotty, the naughtiest dog in the world!

Chapter Eight

Everyone in the hall, including Neil and Mr Hamley, was so shocked, they just stared open-mouthed at the Dalmatian. Dotty stopped barking and gazed round at everyone, her eyes bright with interest.

Meanwhile, Mr Grundy stood on the platform, looking down at the excited dog as if he was hallucinating.

"What . . .?" he spluttered, but he was so taken aback, he couldn't finish the sentence.

Neil was just about to try and grab hold of Dotty, when Mr Hamley finally pulled himself together and hurried forward from the back of the hall. "Dotty!" he said in a trembling voice. "Come here, you naughty girl!"

Dotty bounded towards him, then decided she didn't want her fun cut short just yet. Gleefully she evaded Mr Hamley, and raced towards the platform. Mr Grundy began to back away, looking alarmed, and some of the pupils began to giggle. Neil couldn't help smiling too.

"Dotty!" Mr Hamley shouted, as the dog began to paw happily at the head teacher's spotless trousers. "Come here, *now*!"

Dotty ignored him. Getting tired of Mr Grundy, who wasn't much fun, she jumped down off the platform, and trotted round the other side of the hall. Mr Hamley ran after her, skidding on the highly polished floor. Emily's teacher, Mrs Rowntree, who was at the piano, got up and made a grab for her, but Dotty raced past, obviously having a wonderful time.

"Dotty!" Emily called, as the Dalmatian got closer to where she was sitting with her class. "Come here, girl!"

Dotty hurried over eagerly. Emily grabbed her collar, and hung onto it for all she was worth.

"Well done, Emily!" Mr Hamley called, rushing towards them. "Keep her there!"

That was easier said than done. As Mr Hamley reached them and took the dog's lead from his pocket, Dotty made another determined bid for freedom. She pulled herself away from Emily, and raced to the back of the hall. Mr Hamley followed her, almost tripping over the lead which had fallen to the floor. Most of the pupils had got to their feet to see what was going on more clearly, and the teachers were trying to make them all sit down again. So was Mr Grundy.

"Sit down!" he roared, but no one took any notice.

"This is better than the telly!" Hasheem whispered to Neil.

"Yeah, except Grumpy isn't laughing!"

Suddenly Neil had an idea. He put his hand into his pocket, and pulled out some of the dog treats he always carried. "Here, Dotty!" he called, shaking the packet as the dog came close to him. "Here, girl!"

Dotty stopped in her tracks as she saw the treats, and her eyes lit up. She dashed eagerly over to Neil, who gave her a couple and then grabbed her collar. Chris hurried to help him, and they both hung on to Dotty until Mr Hamley joined them, red in the face. Emily followed, holding Dotty's lead, and the whole school cheered as Mr Hamley finally attached it to Dotty's collar.

"*Silence!*" Mr Grundy shouted. "And *sit down!*" He strode across the floor to where Mr Hamley was desperately clinging on to his mischievous dog. He glared at Mr Hamley, then craned forward and peered at Dotty. "I take it this *animal* is yours, Mr Hamley?"

Mr Hamley nodded, looking deeply embarrassed. Dotty looked up, her eyes sparkling, and leaped eagerly forward to greet this new friend. In the force of Dotty's enthusiastic hello, Mr Grundy lost his balance and landed firmly on his bottom on the hard school floor. As the whole school watched in stunned silence, Dotty planted a paw on their head

teacher's shoulder and gave his cheek a warm, friendly lick.

Mr Grundy looked furiously up at Mr Hamley. "Get that disgusting creature out of *my* school!" he roared. Then he climbed to his feet, extracted a neatly folded handkerchief from his pocket, and wiped his face clean.

Looking shell-shocked, Mr Hamley walked out of the hall with Dotty trotting obediently at his side.

"Do you think he's going to sack Mr Hamley?" Neil whispered to Hasheem, horrified, as the head teacher walked determinedly to the front of the hall. But before Mr Grundy had a chance to say anything, a tall young man with a ponytail and a camera round his neck popped his head round the door. Emily's face lit up when she saw him, and she turned round to glance at Neil a few rows behind her.

"Sorry to interrupt," the man said, "but there's no one in the office."

"And who are you?" Mr Grundy snapped.

"Jake Fielding, *Compton News*." Jake took out his notebook. "Have you got any comment to make about your decision to get rid of the school animals?"

"I think you'd better leave," Mr Grundy said through gritted teeth. "We're in the middle of assembly."

"*Are* you getting rid of the school animals?" Jake asked, flipping through his notebook.

"Yes, he is," Neil said quickly. Mr Grundy shot him an angry glance.

"And there's a petition to try and get you to change your mind, right?" Jake went on.

"Yes, there is!" Emily piped up.

"So will you give me an interview after assembly?" Jake asked again. "Put your side of the story?"

"Certainly not!" Mr Grundy snapped. "Who told you about that ridiculous petition?"

"Sorry, I never reveal my sources."

"Well, I can guess." Mr Grundy's angry gaze swept across the hall, and picked out Neil, Emily and Chris. "You are three of the most undisciplined children it has ever been my misfortune to teach!"

Jake wrote that down in his notebook, and Mr Grundy almost blew a fuse.

"Get off these premises before I call the police," he snapped, and then he eyed Neil, Emily and Chris sternly. "Go and wait in my office, and I'll see you after assembly!"

His tone was venomous, and Neil couldn't help feeling rather afraid. Was the head teacher going to *expel* them, as well as sack Mr Hamley? Things were really getting out of hand, and they hadn't even done anything wrong. Suddenly Neil felt extremely angry. "*No*," he said quietly. "We're not going anywhere."

Mr Grundy looked as if he was going to faint with shock, and Emily turned round again to stare at her brother in amazement. "*What* did you say, Neil Parker?"

"I said no." Neil remained exactly where he was sitting on the floor. "We haven't done anything wrong. All we wanted to do was keep our pets, and we're not moving until you reconsider!"

"Is this a demonstration?" Jake Fielding asked, focusing his camera. "Cool!"

"Neil, d'you know what you're doing?" Hasheem whispered in his ear.

Neil shrugged. He was trembling with fear at the action he'd taken, but he'd had enough of Mr Grundy riding roughshod over everyone's feelings. This was the only thing left that he could think of.

"No pictures!" Mr Grundy yelled at Jake. Then he turned to the rest of the school.

"Assembly has been cancelled," he announced. "Stand up, please."

No one moved.

"Stand up, please!" Mr Grundy shouted, but again no one moved.

"Looks to me like the demonstration's spread to the whole school," Jake remarked. "Have you got any comment *now*, Mr Grundy?"

"No," muttered the head teacher, who had turned pale. He stared helplessly at the rows of pupils around him, and Neil felt his heart pounding with a mixture of fear and delight. Everyone in the school was supporting them! Surely Mr Grundy couldn't ignore the *whole school*?

"I order you all to stand *up*!" the head teacher roared. "This insubordination won't get you anywhere!"

"What's going on here?" asked a surprised voice, and a tall, middle-aged man in horn-rimmed spectacles walked into the hall. Neil glanced at Chris and Emily and raised his eyebrows. It was Mr Bingham, the chairman of the school governors! Mr Grundy took one look at him, and collapsed like a burst balloon. "Hello, Mr Bingham," he blustered nervously. "I, er . . . wasn't expecting you this morning."

"So I see," Mr Bingham remarked acidly.

"We're protesting about Mr Grundy taking away our classroom pets, sir," Neil said quickly before the head teacher had a chance to say anything.

Mr Bingham raised his eyebrows. "Really? Well, that's why I'm here. I had a call from the *Compton News* this morning, asking me for my reaction to this news."

"That was me," Jake put in, still writing furiously.

"So, as I didn't know anything about it," Mr Bingham went on, "I thought I'd better come and find out." He eyed the head teacher sternly. "Perhaps we ought to go and have a talk in your office, Mr Grundy. Meanwhile," he looked at Neil, "I think you should all go back to class, while we discuss the issue of the school animals in more detail."

That was good enough for Neil. He climbed to his feet, and so did everyone else. As they all filed out, Neil felt his legs shaking so much he could hardly walk. Although it looked like he might have got away with it, he could have been in serious trouble for disobeying the head teacher.

"Brilliant move, Neil!" Hasheem slapped Neil

on the back as they went into the classroom. "You really showed old Grumpy up!"

The rest of Mr Hamley's class broke into spontaneous applause, and Neil turned pink.

"I didn't do anything much," he muttered. "Anyway, we still don't know what's going to happen to Mr Hamley."

The class fell silent.

"Looks like old Smiler might be out on his ear," Hasheem said solemnly.

Neil nodded. They would no doubt find out Mr Hamley's fate, as well as that of the school animals, soon enough. But at the moment, all they could do was wait.

The rest of the morning was difficult. Because Mr Hamley was absent, Neil's class was split up and sent to other classrooms to work. He was on edge all the time, and couldn't concentrate. At lunchtime he met up with Chris, and they went to the classroom to see if Mr Hamley had come back. He hadn't.

While they were there, Emily came in.

"I just wanted to see what had happened to Mr Hamley," she said anxiously.

"We don't know, but his stuff's still here." Neil pointed at the books and papers strewn over the teacher's desk. "That's a good sign."

"D'you really think Grumpy will sack him?" Emily asked.

Neil wondered how Mr Hamley would cope if he did get the sack, what with the new baby and Dotty and her puppies to look after. "We'll have to wait and see."

They didn't have to wait much longer, though, because just then the teacher walked into the classroom, a sheaf of papers in his hand. "What are you three doing in here?" he asked. "You should be outside." But he didn't really look angry.

"How's Dotty, Mr Hamley?" Neil asked. He'd never thought he'd be so happy to see Smiler again.

"All that excitement didn't tire her out, if that's what you're worried about!" Mr Hamley said, with a wry smile.

"You're not leaving, are you?" Emily asked.

Mr Hamley shook his head, looking embarrassed. "Mr Bingham's sorted everything out," he said quickly. "Now off you go to lunch."

"Has anything been decided about the school animals, sir?" Emily asked in a determined voice.

Mr Hamley hesitated, then gave her one of

the sheets of paper he was holding. Neil saw that it was another letter to take home to their parents.

"*There has been a re-think concerning the decision to remove the classroom animals,*" Emily read. "*There have been several objections to the plan, so it has been decided that the animals will remain in school for the foreseeable future.*

"Yes!" Emily punched the air triumphantly, and Neil and Chris grinned at each other. It had been a long struggle, but they'd finally won!

"You're staying, Tom and Jerry!" Neil said, bending over the gerbils' cage.

"I'm sure they're very pleased," said Mr Hamley drily, beginning to look more like his old self every minute. "Now will you *please* go outside?"

"I knew we'd do it!" Emily crowed as they hurried out.

"Maybe from now on Grumpy'll take some notice of us!" Chris added.

Neil nodded, but, although he was just as pleased as the other two, he was secretly a little nervous about how Mr Grundy would treat *him* in future. Because, after that demonstration in the school hall, he was now a marked man as far as the head teacher was concerned.

Chapter Nine

"That was the Carters." Bob put the phone down, looking grim. "They'll be here in twenty minutes to collect Duke."

Neil, who had just walked into the office, felt himself go cold all over. "Did you tell them what happened?"

Bob shook his head.

"It's better done face to face. I'm going to ring Sergeant Moorhead and get him here straight-away. Could you go and find your mother, Neil?"

Carole Parker was in the rescue centre, kneeling down outside Star's pen. The shaggy little dog was pressed right up against the fence, enjoying all the attention Carole was giving him. Neil smiled to himself as he stopped in the doorway to watch. Star was certainly helping his mother to rediscover her love of dogs, he thought, pleased. But she still hadn't plucked up courage to go inside the pen.

Carole hadn't noticed that Neil was there. She stood up, and brushed herself down as Star continued to paw at the fence. Then she reached into her pocket and took out a bunch of keys.

Neil's heart began to hammer with excitement as he saw his mother unlock the door of Star's pen. She hesitated for a moment. Then she pushed the door open and went in. Star barked happily, and flung himself at Carole, climbing up onto her knees as she knelt down, and licking her face. Carole took the dog in her arms and hugged it lovingly as Neil hurried towards them. He was thrilled, but he wasn't going to say so. His mum obviously wanted to pretend that nothing had been wrong.

Carole looked up and saw him as she tickled Star's tummy. "And what have you been up to, Neil Parker?" she asked, eyebrows raised.

Neil didn't know what she meant, until Carole walked over to Star's basket and picked up her sweatshirt. Then Neil remembered that he'd

forgotten to take it with him when he'd sneaked into Star's pen earlier that morning. The little dog must have dragged it into his basket. "I was just trying to help," he muttered sheepishly.

Carole came out of Star's pen, and gave him a quick hug. "Thanks," was all she said, but Neil knew that she'd guessed what he had done, and they smiled at each other. He couldn't wait to tell Emily that now everything would be back to normal.

Then, with a sickening jolt, Neil remembered why he was there. "The Carters are on their way to collect Duke."

Carole nodded. "We'd better go and wait for them then."

Sergeant Moorhead had just arrived, and was in the office with Bob.

"Dad, can I stay while you talk to the Carters?" Neil asked. He really wanted to know what was going to happen to Duke.

His father hesitated, then nodded. "All right, Neil, but you're to keep quiet, OK?" He glanced out of the window as a red car pulled onto the driveway. "Here they are."

Neil felt sick as he watched Mr and Mrs Carter getting out of their car. He tried to imagine how *he* would feel if he and Sam were in the same situation as the Carters and Duke. It didn't bear thinking about.

Bob went out to meet the couple, and escorted them into the office. The Carters saw Sergeant Moorhead, and stopped short in the doorway.

"What's going on?" Mr Carter asked, swallowing nervously. He was a short man with glasses and grey hair.

"I'm afraid we've had some trouble with Duke—" Bob began, but that was as far as he got. To everyone's horror, Mrs Carter immediately burst into tears.

"What sort of trouble?" Mr Carter asked, as Carole handed his wife a tissue. His gaze fell on Carole's bandaged hand, and he turned pale. "Has Duke . . .?" But he couldn't finish the sentence.

"Duke bit my wife very badly," Bob said. "I take it this isn't the first time he's done it?"

Mr Carter hesitated.

"It's best to be honest about these things, Mr Carter," Sergeant Moorhead said gently.

"Duke's always been a bit aggressive," Mr Carter muttered, his face pale. "Not to us, but to people he doesn't know very well."

"What's his history?" Bob asked.

"We don't know. He's a stray we found a couple of years ago."

"And he's done this before?"

Neil waited on tenterhooks for the Carters to reply.

Mr Carter nodded reluctantly. "He's bitten our daughter, and a neighbour. And—"

At that point Mr Carter's wife nudged him and he stopped abruptly.

"Tell us exactly how many people Duke has bitten," Sergeant Moorhead persisted.

"Five," Mr Carter admitted reluctantly. "Well . . ." He glanced at Carole. "Six."

"But he's always fine with us," Mrs Carter said tearfully. "He's a real softie."

"You should have told us, Mr Carter." Neil could tell his father was furious, even though he spoke calmly. "Your dog could have attacked one of my children."

The Carters looked stricken.

"Sorry," Mr Carter stammered. "We didn't think of that."

"Do you have grandchildren?" Sergeant Moorhead asked. The Carters nodded.

"And are you happy about Duke being around them?"

"Well, no . . ." Mr Carter shuffled his feet, looking embarrassed. "Our daughter won't let the kids come round unless Duke's locked in the garden shed, because once he . . ." Then he stopped.

"You mean the dog's gone for one of your *grandchildren*?" Carole asked, horrified.

"He didn't mean it," Mr Carter said weakly, but even he didn't look convinced.

"I'm going to speak plainly, Mr Carter," Bob said quietly. "A dog who has bitten people so many times is dangerous; especially as we don't know his history. If Duke was younger, I might have suggested some sort of behaviour therapy, but as it is . . ."

Neil took a sharp intake of breath.

Bob Parker paused, then went on very gently: "The only sensible and kind solution would be to have Duke put down."

Mrs Carter burst into tears again, and Mr Carter didn't look far off an outburst of emotion either.

"But you – you can't force us to do that?" he asked in a trembling voice.

Bob shook his head. "No one's forcing you to do anything," he assured them. "But Sergeant Moorhead has recommended that if you don't agree, the matter should be taken to court to let

the magistrate decide. With Duke's history, it's likely that a destruction order will be granted."

"We *have* discussed this before." Mr Carter looked anguished. "We know Duke's unpredictable. We hoped he would just calm down."

Bob shook his head. "It's gone too far for that."

Neil watched silently, wondering what the Carters would decide to do.

"He's right, you know, Daphne," Mr Carter said miserably, taking his wife's hands. "We've been putting this off for long enough. It's not fair on us *or* Duke. What if he hurt someone seriously? We'd never forgive ourselves."

Mrs Carter nodded, and wiped her eyes. "Can we see him?" she asked tremulously.

Bob nodded, and he and Sergeant Moorhead led them out of the office. Neil followed them quietly.

Duke was lying in his basket. But as soon as the Carters entered Kennel Block One, he shot to his feet, barking, and began to run around his pen. The transformation was remarkable. The large black mongrel had suddenly come to life again. Neil watched unhappily from the doorway as his father let the Carters in.

"Hello, boy!" Mr Carter said in a strained voice, kneeling down to stroke Duke. Mrs

Carter flung her arms round the dog's neck.

Neil felt a lump come into his throat. It must be dreadful to know that the dog you loved was going to be put to sleep. He suddenly thought of Sam, and he had to blink hard to stop the tears. His mother came up quietly behind him, and slid an arm round his shoulders.

"Horrible, isn't it?" she said in a low voice. "But it's for the best, Neil. Duke is too unpredictable."

"I know," Neil muttered.

"And I've got some good news that might cheer you up," Carole went on. "A Miss Sanderson just phoned. She thinks Star might be her dog."

"That's great." But although Neil was glad that Star might be reunited with his owner, he still couldn't help feeling bad about Duke who wouldn't be going home ever again.

"*What?* I don't believe it!" Neil stared at Hasheem, his eyes wide with amazement. "Is this one of your jokes, Hasheem? Because if it is . . ."

"No joke!" Hasheem shook his head. "Mr Grundy's resigned! It's all over the school!"

Neil had had a difficult weekend. Although his mother was now back to normal and Star (real name Dougal) had been returned to his delighted owner, the removal of Duke to Mike Turner's surgery to be put to sleep had affected everyone at King Street badly. Now Neil could hardly take in what Hasheem was telling him. Mr Grundy was leaving? It didn't seem possible.

"How do you know, Hasheem?" he asked cautiously.

"Kathy Jones told me!"

"And how does *she* know?" Neil persisted.

"Someone else told her, I suppose!" Hasheem grinned. "Maybe he didn't want to wait for the *Compton News* to come out on Friday and make him look like a real idiot!"

"Well, I won't believe it until it's official," Neil said. Then he saw Mr Hamley walking into the playground with Dotty trotting along beside him.

"Maybe it *is* true!" Chris nudged Neil. "I don't think Smiler would be bringing Dotty to school if Mr Grundy was still here."

"Sir!" Neil ran over to Mr Hamley. "Is it true that Mr Grundy's leaving?"

Mr Hamley looked taken aback. "Who told you that?" Then he smiled reluctantly. "It's impossible to keep anything a secret in this school! Yes, it's true. Mr Grundy has decided to look for a post at another school."

Neil knew that Hasheem and Chris were thinking the same thing as he was. *Good riddance!*

"Under the circumstances, Mr Bingham said it was all right for me to keep Dotty in the boiler room," Mr Hamley went on. "So I'd be very grateful if you could help me to keep an eye on her. Officially this time."

"We'd love to, sir!" Neil agreed, patting Dotty's sleek head.

"I, er . . . have to meet with the governors at lunchtime, so if you could spend some time with Dotty then?" Mr Hamley barely had time to finish the sentence before Dotty lunged forward, barking at the top of her voice. Everyone turned to see Mr Grundy, his arms full of folders and books, hurrying across the playground as if he couldn't get out of the place fast enough.

"D'you think we should say goodbye?" Hasheem asked cheekily.

"That's enough, Hasheem," Mr Hamley said sternly. But Neil could tell that the teacher was relieved too.

Mr Grundy was glaring at them as he came closer, obviously planning to stalk past them with his nose in the air. But Dotty had other ideas. As Mr Grundy approached, she bounded forward to say hello.

"Get off!" Mr Grundy roared. He leaped backwards to avoid the Dalmatian, then staggered and fell, dropping everything he was carrying. Neil could hardly keep a straight face as he, Hasheem and Chris went to help the ex-head teacher pick his belongings up.

"I'm sorry, Mr Grundy," Mr Hamley apologized, but Mr Grundy, who was fishing one of his books out of a puddle, ignored him. Red-faced with fury, he grabbed everything from the three boys without so much as a thank-you. Then he stamped across the playground, jumped into his car and drove off.

"I think he's as glad to see the back of us as we are to see the back of him!" Chris said, as Mr Hamley took Dotty into school.

"Yeah, I wonder who'll take over now?" Hasheem remarked.

"Didn't you hear what Mr Hamley said?" Neil pointed out. "He's got a meeting with the governors today. I bet Smiler's being interviewed for the head's job again!"

"Well, let's hope he gets it this time!" Hasheem remarked. "Or we might end up with another Grumpy Grundy!"

*

Although Neil was sure that Mr Hamley's "meeting" with the governors was in fact an interview, Mr Hamley did not refer to it all morning. He worked the class hard right up until lunchtime, but nobody complained. The atmosphere all round the school felt a lot happier now Mr Grundy had gone.

"Have you heard?" Emily yelled happily as she raced up to Neil and Chris in the corridor.

"Yes, we've heard!" Neil grinned at her. "And we reckon Smiler's up for the job!"

"Really?" Emily looked pleased.

Just then Hasheem ran to catch them up. "Are you going to see Dotty now?" he asked.

Neil explained to Emily that they were keeping an eye on Dotty while Mr Hamley was with the governors, and she decided to go to the boiler room with them.

"I'm going to keep my fingers crossed that Mr Hamley gets the job," Emily remarked as they went down the corridor to the boiler room.

"He deserves it." Neil pulled the door open. "He's had some pretty bad luck lately. Hello, Dotty! Dotty?"

Neil and the others stared into the boiler room. The dog basket was empty.

Dotty had vanished.

Chapter Ten

"**W**here *is* she?" Emily gasped. A swift search of the room had revealed nothing.

"We've got to find her!" Neil said. "She must be somewhere around the school!" They all hurried back along the corridor, keeping a sharp lookout for Dotty, and checking all the classrooms on the ground floor. There were no children in there because everyone had gone for lunch, but there were no dogs either. They looked inside the gym too, but it was deserted.

"Maybe she's gone to find Mr Hamley," Hasheem suggested.

"But he's having an interview in the school hall!" Chris said. "If Dotty had turned up there, he would've brought her straight back."

"You don't think she might have gone outside?" Emily asked, her face pale with worry. "She might even have managed to get out of the playground!"

Neil was thinking hard. "I'm sure Dotty would have gone wherever she scented Mr Hamley," he said slowly, "and if she didn't go to the hall—"

"She could have gone to your classroom!" Chris broke in. "Neil, you're a genius!"

They all raced for the stairs, Neil in front and taking them two at a time. They hurried into Mr Hamley's room, and looked around.

The classroom, which always looked bigger when there were no children in it, seemed empty. Apart from the rows of tables and chairs, there was a bigger desk near the window where Mr Hamley sat. Then Emily clutched Neil's arm.

"Look!"

Dotty was lying underneath the teacher's table next to the waste-paper bin. Mr Hamley's overcoat had been thrown over the back of his chair, and the Dalmatian, recognizing the scent, had dragged it off and made herself a nest on the floor. Alarmed, Neil saw that Dotty was on her side, panting, and that every so often her bulging stomach moved, as if the puppies inside were impatient to be born. He turned to the others. "Dotty's having her pups!"

"*What*?" Hasheem gasped. "Now?"

"Puppies don't wait for the right moment," Neil said grimly. He checked Dotty again. He didn't think she was ready to give birth immediately, but it could be quite soon. "Hasheem, go and ask the secretary to phone Mike Turner, and I'll fetch Mr Hamley."

"But you said he was having an interview!" Chris said.

"That's just too bad!" Neil ran out of the door, and along the corridor. Dotty was more important than any interview. And he knew that Mr Hamley would feel the same.

When Neil got to the school hall, the doors were closed, but he knocked and went straight in. Mr Hamley was sitting in front of a long table, with all the school governors, including Mr Bingham, grouped around it.

". . . and I have plenty of ideas to make the school a more attractive and child-friendly place if I'm appointed head teacher," Mr Hamley was saying. "For instance—"

"Sorry to interrupt, sir," Neil blurted out as everyone, including Mr Hamley, glared at him, "but Dotty's pups are on their way!"

Mr Hamley's face changed. "But they're early!" Then he pulled himself together quickly, and jumped up. "I'm afraid I'll have to leave," he said to Mr Bingham. The chairman looked astonished. "I see. You do realize, Mr Hamley, that this will affect your application?"

The teacher nodded. "I'm very sorry, but I must go."

"I didn't mean to interrupt," Neil apologized as they left the hall.

"Don't worry." Neil was glad to hear that the

teacher sounded sincere. "I couldn't let Dotty go through this alone."

There was now quite a crowd in the classroom when Neil and Mr Hamley got back, as more pupils had come inside to see what was going on. Neil was glad to see that they were all sitting quietly, so as not to upset Dotty, and that Chris and Emily had moved some of the chairs and tables, as well as the waste-paper basket, to give Dotty some space. He took a quick look at the Dalmatian, and saw that the contractions of her abdomen were coming more quickly. It looked like she was already in the second stage of labour.

"I think she's in the second stage," Mr Hamley said confidently, kneeling down to examine Dotty. He flushed slightly as Neil looked amazed. "I've been reading up on it," he explained, "and I helped my sister deliver her bitch's puppies a few months ago."

"How long will it be before the puppies are born, sir?" asked Julie Baker, one of Emily's friends.

"Not long," Mr Hamley said, and there was a ripple of excitement round the room. "See how Dotty's sides are heaving as the puppies move down the birth canal?"

"Did the secretary call Mike?" Neil whispered to Hasheem.

Hasheem nodded. "He's out on another job, but he'll get here as soon as he can."

Everyone listened intently as Mr Hamley explained how the puppies would be born. Even Neil was surprised by how knowledgeable he was. The teacher had brought some old towels to school with him, and he placed some of them round Dotty's hindquarters.

"I may need to clean up the puppies myself when they're born," he told the watching crowd. "Sometimes the mother isn't quite sure what to do. Ah, here comes the first one!"

Dotty panted hard, and pushed, and a small bundle began to appear, wrapped in a transparent bag. Dotty gave an extra push, and the bundle slid out onto the towel. The pupils, who'd never seen this before, gasped in amazement.

"Yuck!" Julie whispered. "What's all that stuff around the puppy?"

"That's just the bag that protects the puppy while it's growing inside the mother," Mr Hamley explained quickly. "And see the cord? That feeds the puppy until it's born."

Neil wondered if the Dalmatian was going to

need help to break the bag open and release the puppy, like Delilah had when her puppies were born. But Dotty instinctively reached out and gently broke the bag with her teeth. A clear liquid poured out and for the first time they could all see the tiny white puppy more clearly.

"But it hasn't got any spots!" Hasheem gasped.

Mr Hamley smiled. "The spots will appear later as it gets older. Now we've got to make sure that we clear this little one's airways so that he can breathe." He glanced at Neil. "Would you like to do the honours? You're probably more of an expert than I am!"

Thrilled, Neil carefully took the puppy from the teacher. It wriggled as he gently cleaned its face.

"Well done, Dotty!" Neil murmured. He put the puppy down close to its mother's tummy, and it floundered around for a moment before latching on to one of her teats, to feed.

"How many puppies will she have, sir?" Chris asked.

"Dalmatians can have quite a few pups in one litter," Mr Hamley replied. "Anything from seven upwards."

Suddenly he stopped and glanced towards the door. The governors were standing in the doorway, watching what was going on.

"Please carry on!" Mr Bingham said with a smile. "We're enjoying the lesson as much as the children obviously are."

Mr Hamley looked uncertain, but Neil leaped in to distract him. "I think another pup's on the way!" he said urgently.

"Right." Mr Hamley forgot all about the governors, and bent over Dotty again. "Come on, girl. You can do it!"

"Eight puppies!" Emily said ecstatically, as she, Neil and Chris walked up the Hamleys' path. "Can you believe it?"

"I don't think the governors could!" Neil laughed. "Their eyes almost popped out along with the puppies!"

Everything had gone without a hitch. Mike Turner had arrived just before the last puppy was born, and had praised Mr Hamley's calm handling of the situation. He had also helped the teacher to transport Dotty and her newborn offspring back home. It wasn't considered a good idea to move a new mother and her pups, but Mike had felt it was worth the risk to get

Dotty back into familiar surroundings, and restore order to the classroom. Mr Hamley had been very grateful to Neil and the others, and had told them to call in for a few minutes after school if they wanted to have another quick look at the puppies.

"Ah, here you are!" beamed Mr Hamley as he opened the door. "Come in, Dotty's expecting you!"

Neil grinned. He'd never seen Smiler looking *quite* so smiley!

Mrs Hamley had just arrived back from Manchester and was sitting on the sofa with the baby on her knee, while Dotty was lying in her basket in front of the fire. The Dalmatian was dozing, but she opened her eyes and wagged her tail proudly as they went in. The puppies were snuggled up against their mother's warm tummy, all fast asleep.

"She's just fed them," Mrs Hamley said proudly, "so they're *all* tired out!"

"Aren't they beautiful?" Emily knelt down, and gently scratched the nearest pup's head. He snuffled a little, but didn't wake up.

"I'm sorry about your interview, Mr Hamley," Neil said, patting Dotty.

"Oh, that." Mr Hamley didn't look very

worried at all. "Well, maybe you'll find out tomorrow just who your new head teacher is . . ."

"You mean you got the job?" Neil gasped.

Mr Hamley shrugged. "I didn't say that, did I?" The doorbell rang, and he went out. "Must be some more of your admirers, Dotty!"

"He *did* get the job!" Neil whispered to the others. "The governors must have been impressed with the way he handled the birth of the puppies!"

"Well, I learnt a lot for sure!" Chris agreed.

Mr Hamley came back with Neil's parents and Sarah.

"We just had to come and see Dotty's pups," Carole explained, as they all gathered round the basket. "Everyone's talking about the dramatic way they arrived!"

Mr Hamley smiled. "I'm just glad that Neil fetched me so promptly."

Neil looked down at the sleeping pups. Everything had turned out all right in the end. Except for Duke, he thought, his heart sinking just for a moment. Duke had been a tiny puppy like this once.

But Neil knew that life had to go on. And, if the pups turned out to be anything like their mother, there was a whole lot of fun, as well as chaos, ahead!

"Well done, Dotty!" he said, stroking the Dalmatian's glossy black ears. "I think you're going to make a brilliant mum!"